MYSTERY IN
THE FROZEN LANDS

MYSTERY IN THE FROZEN LANDS

MARTYN GODFREY

James Lorimer & Company, Publishers
Toronto 1988

Canadian Cataloguing in Publication Data

Godfrey, Martyn
Mystery in the frozen lands

(Adventures in Canadian history)

ISBN 1-55028-144-5 (bound)
1-55028-137-2 (pbk.)

1. Fox (Ship) - Juvenile fiction. 2. Franklin, John,
Sir,1786-1847 - Juvenile fiction. 3. Arctic regions -
Juvenile fiction. I. Title. II. Series.

PS8563.08165M961988   jC813'.54
C88-094852-3   PZ7.G63My 1988

1-55028-137-2 paper
1-55028-144-5 cloth

Cover Illustration: Don Besco

Maps: Dave Hunter

James Lorimer & Company, Publishers
Egerton Ryerson Memorial Building
35 Britain Street.
Toronto, Ontario M5A 1R7

To Dr. Roger Amy and his family, with thanks for the help and the interesting conversations

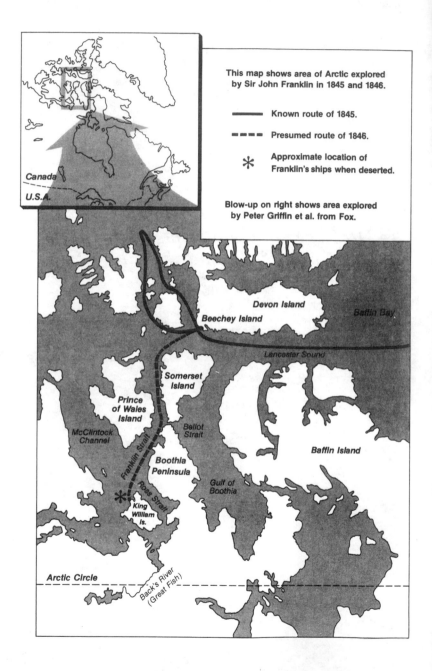

This map shows area of Arctic explored by Sir John Franklin in 1845 and 1846.

———— Known route of 1845.

---- Presumed route of 1846.

* Approximate location of Franklin's ships when deserted.

Blow-up on right shows area explored by Peter Griffin et al. from Fox.

Canada

U.S.A.

Devon Island

Beechey Island

Baffin Bay

Lancaster Sound

Somerset Island

Prince of Wales Island

Bellot Strait

McClintock Channel

Franklin Strait

Boothia Peninsula

Baffin Island

Ross Strait

Gulf of Boothia

* King William Is.

Arctic Circle

Back's River (Great Fish)

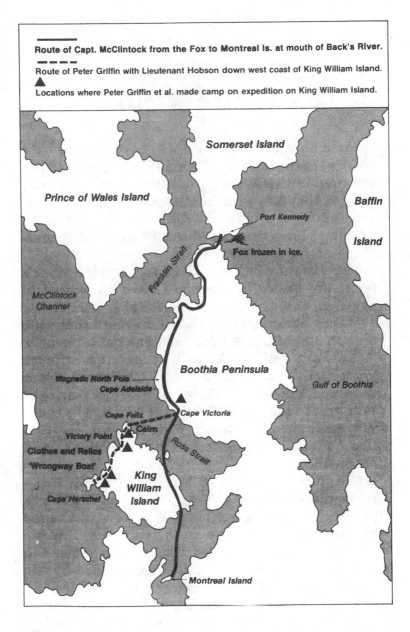

Route of Capt. McClintock from the Fox to Montreal Is. at mouth of Back's River.

Route of Peter Griffin with Lieutenant Hobson down west coast of King William Island.

▲ Locations where Peter Griffin et al. made camp on expedition on King William Island.

Somerset Island

Prince of Wales Island

Baffin

Island

Port Kennedy

Fox frozen in ice.

Franklin Strait

McClintock Channel

Boothia Peninsula

Gulf of Boothia

Magnetic North Pole
Cape Adelaide

▲

Cape Felix   Cape Victoria

Victory Point   Cairn

Clothes and Relics
'Wrongway Boat'

▲

Ross Strait

▲

King
William
Island

Cape Herschel

Montreal Island

Author's Note

No doubt an Arctic historian will be concerned with the representation of some historical details presented in this work of fiction. To the purists, I ask that they keep in mind that it is fiction for a young audience and not a scholarly account. So, for example, I have used the term "Inuit" when referring to native northerners.

The events of Captain Francis McClintock's voyage are basically correct. I have attempted to organize the time frame of Peter Griffith's adventure according to the exact events that took place on and off the *Fox*. Peter was not a member of the *Fox*'s crew. All other crew and officers mentioned, including Anton Christian from Greenland, served on the vessel. The discoveries of the cairn at Victory Point and the "wrongway" boat were made by Lieutenant W.R. Hobson. Captain Allen Young was exploring Prince of Wales Island in May, 1859.

The questions that still puzzled Peter Griffin — why would the crews of the *Erebus* and the *Terror* carry such unusual articles if they were weakened by starvation, Crozier's note, why the officers' deaths were out of proportion to the crew, the skeletons, and so on — could be explained by the theory that lead poisoning may have affected the Franklin Expedition. Solder on the cans used by the Franklin Expedition may have tainted the food, and subsequently poisoned the officers and crew.

Among the symptoms of lead poisoning is mental confusion.

This theory is presented by Dr. Owen Beattie of the University of Alberta. He has led his own expeditions to Beechey Island to do research on the three crewmen buried during the winter of 1845-46. His conclusions can be read in the work *Frozen In Time: Unlocking the Secrets of the Franklin Expedition*, Owen Beattie, John Geiger, published by Western Producer Prairie Books.

There is little doubt that scurvy had a major impact on the health of Arctic explorers, including the crews of the Franklin Expedition and the *Fox*. The symptoms of scurvy — the lack of sufficient Vitamin C in the diet — include backaches, muscle cramps, bleeding gums, tooth loss, re-opening of scar tissue and depression. Although sailors of this time were aware that certain foods helped prevent the condition, they did not understand why. Vitamin C is fairly fragile, and sources such as lemon juice would lose their potency with time. It was believed that cleanliness and exercise were also necessary in the prevention of scurvy.

A special acknowledgement goes to Dr. Roger Amy, pathologist at the University of Alberta Hospital, for giving me the idea for this book and for his valuable assistance. Also, thanks to the Alberta Foundation for the Literary Arts for their generous support.

1

November 10, 1858. Aboard the Fox, *frozen in the ice off Port Kennedy, Bellot Strait.*

George Brand, our engineer, is dead. Four days ago he placed a musket under his chin and pulled the trigger.

Why did he kill himself? Was it a stroke, as Dr. Walker said? Below deck, the crew believes that Brand took his own life because he thought that death was more inviting than another winter in this frozen land. That may be true. I can understand how thoughts of the long darkness and the numbing cold could become too much to bear.

The sun vanished a few days ago, leaving just a feeble glow in the southern sky. In another week even that will disappear — two months of night.

After Brand's funeral this morning, I brought tea to Captain McClintock's cabin. I knocked and squeezed through the door. The Captain shuffled the books on his desk to make room for the tray.

"Warm scones, sir," I announced. "Cook just took a batch from the oven. And I've opened a can of gooseberry preserve."

"Delightful," the Captain smiled. "Mr. Shingleton's cakes are always welcome. When you go back below deck, you may take a can of preserves for the crew. Maybe it will lighten the spirits of this sad day."

"Yes, sir." I lifted the silver pot and poured dark tea into the Captain's china cup.

The Captain swirled his spoon in the pot of sweet golden syrup and then dropped it into the cup. "Why the long face, boy?"

I shrugged. "It's nothing, sir."

Captain McClintock shook his head slowly and began to spread the gooseberry jam on the scone. "Don't lie. I won't tolerate that. Heavy lips and eyes mean a heavy heart. What's wrong?"

"Well, sir, it's the death of Mr. Brand. The crew thinks it was the thought of winter that made him do it. I've been thinking that myself."

Captain McClintock placed the half-eaten scone on the tray. "Rubbish! Mr. Brand didn't kill himself because he was thinking about the Arctic winter. Mr. Brand killed himself because he was seriously ill. Dr. Walker said that Mr. Brand suffered apoplexy, a stroke to his brain."

"Yes, but — "

"Don't start brooding," he grumbled. "Perhaps I don't keep you busy enough. Perhaps I should find more chores for you." He examined the teapot. "Maybe you should clean the silverware every day."

"I'm more than busy, sir," I said quickly. The last thing I need is more duties.

"Just the same." He reached into the top drawer of his desk and handed me a book of blank paper. "Here. I know you can write. I want you to start a journal. Record the events of the coming months. We're close to our goal now. We're on the verge of solving the great mystery."

I stared at the empty book.

"Keeping a journal will put your thoughts in order. It will stop you from brooding. That's an order, Peter. Keep a journal. Now, go and be busy."

And so, on Captain's orders, I begin this journal.

My name is Peter Griffin of Somerset. My fourteenth birthday was three weeks ago. I am the son of Robert Griffin, former Lieutenant in the British Navy, First Mate under Captain McClure of the *H.M.S. Investigator* and brother of Lady Jane Franklin. My father died in 1855 of pneumonia. My mother, Helen, died a year earlier giving birth to my sister, Rachel.

I am ship's boy on the *Fox*. We sailed from Aberdeen, Scotland, sixteen months ago, on July 2, 1857. The purpose of our voyage is to discover the fate of Sir John Franklin's Expedition of 1845. We are in the Arctic searching for my uncle and the one hundred twenty-eight men under his command. They have been missing for thirteen years.

There are twenty-six of us aboard the *Fox*...no, that's not true. There are *twenty-five* of us. George Brand now sleeps in frozen ground.

Mr. Brand is our second death. Our first happened last winter when Robert Scott, our stoker, fell down the upper hatchway. For his burial, we cut a hole in the ice and dropped the body into the sea.

Last winter...

The ship froze in the pack ice of Baffin Bay last year, far, far from shore. The days spent in that long darkness were unpleasant indeed. The cramped life aboard the *Fox* and a terrible homesickness lowered my spirits for many weeks.

I would wake in the middle of the night sobbing. What was I doing in the middle of this frigid, lifeless blackness? How many more months would pass before the air warmed and the ice melted?

Were such memories on Brand's mind when he pulled the trigger? They are strong in my thoughts now. But I could never do what Brand did — no matter how bad our circumstances. Being buried in the ever-frozen dirt would be far more horrible than even the pitiful state of our lives.

I was the last to see George Brand alive. I knocked on his door at nine o'clock, entered his tiny cabin and stoked the stove with fresh coal. He was on his bed, reading. He did not speak to me, but that was not unusual. Brand seldom spoke to anyone from below deck, unless it was to give an order.

After completing my chores, I left the officers' deck and went down to my hammock. Most of the crew were asleep, and only one light still flickered. The air was thick with the oily stench of the lamps and the musk of body odour. In the semi-darkness, I threaded my way through the hammocks and accidentally bumped someone. The figure swore and threw out an arm to cuff me, but I was fast enough to dodge the swing. I inched more carefully toward the back of the deck and hooked my hammock between two storage crates.

It took me a long time to fall asleep. The wind was tearing at the canvas housing, trying to push its long, cold tentacles inside. The wood snapped and groaned in protest.

When I did sleep, I dreamed I was walking across the pack ice. The ice was rough and jagged and I kept stumbling. I had been hunting for seal and was returning to the *Fox*, but I couldn't find her. My eyes strained to see the outline of the ship in the dark of the Arctic day. Nothing. And then suddenly, a hole opened in the ice and I slipped into the black liquid. I tried to claw my way back onto the ice, but the water seeped through my parka and I slowly drifted into the murk, the cold sea swallowing me.

The shot from George Brand's musket woke me from that dream.

The next morning, I helped Dr. Walker prepare Brand's body. We washed him, trimmed his hair and dressed him in his best shirt and trousers. Dr. Walker tied cotton strips around his arms, thighs and big toes to keep the limbs in place. I sewed a cotton shroud around the body.

"Made a nasty mess of himself, didn't he?" Dr. Walker observed.

"Why would he do that?" I asked.

"Apoplexy." The doctor pointed to his forehead. "Sudden bleeding in the brain."

"But I thought people who had such a stroke died quickly."

"Most of the time," he agreed. "But there are cases when a person will behave strangely. What else can it be?"

What else...?

The darkness.

The ice.

The cold.

The frozen land.

After we'd finished preparing Brand's body, we moved it to the top deck so that the body would freeze.

We had to do this because it took four days to dig the grave. Dig isn't the proper word. We had to pick at the ground and dislodge each pebble from the frozen soil. Even in the height of summer, the ground remains frozen.

George Edwards, the carpenter's mate, made a fine coffin of mahogany, and a brass plaque with Brand's name and dates was nailed on the lid.

The funeral service began under the housing on the top deck. After the hymns, the body was placed on a sledge and dragged across the ice to the shore.

The lanterns barely made a dent in the gloom. The pink glow in the southern sky gave no warmth, but the moon cast a wide halo in the misty air. At six points of the halo were false moons — bright reflections of the white planet.

The cold froze my breath on my fur hood. It crawled through the jagged angles of the ice and oozed from the black jaw of the grave.

When Captain McClintock committed Brand's body to the ground, it wasn't the earth that claimed him. It was the cold.

Tonight I am going to pray that I will keep my strength. I don't want to die in this forsaken part of the world. I don't want to be lowered into the frozen gravel that serves as soil in these lands.

I will try not to think that spring is still a half year away.

2

November 12, 1858. Aboard the Fox, *frozen in the ice off Port Kennedy, Bellot Strait.*

The temperature is fairly mild, minus 27, but a sharp, damp breeze has been blowing for the past three days, making it unpleasant to go outside.

I have just finished my housekeeping and laundry chores on the upper deck. Now that we are wearing our winter clothes again, lice are more of a problem. Captain McClintock has ordered me to wash the officers' bedding every second day in an attempt to keep their numbers down. Dr. Walker insists that we wash ourselves and trim our hair often. He tells us that keeping clean is the first step toward preventing scurvy.

Despite the foul weather, the crew has off-loaded some of the supplies onto the ice, so we now have more room below deck. This is a great luxury.

When I first came aboard the *Fox*, I was shocked by how tiny she was. I was expecting her to be at least the size of a Navy ship or steamer. Instead, I discovered that I'd signed aboard a tiny, refitted yacht. After she was fully loaded, there was barely room to take a deep breath.

The five officers bunk on the first deck — four now that Mr. Brand is dead. Their cabins are mere pigeon-holes. Even in the Captain's room there is only enough space to stand between his bed and desk. Their mess-room is but eight feet square and the rest of their deck is crammed with supplies.

The crew, twenty-one of us, sleep on the lower deck. The Able-Bodied Seamen enjoy the relative comfort of a wall bunk, while everyone else uses a hammock. The smallness of the ship means that supplies are stored on our deck as well. We sleep by stringing hammocks between the crates.

Except for our interpreter, Mr. Petersen, the crew only visit the officers on ship's business. And the officers seldom come below deck unless it's on a specific errand.

Our living quarters are stifling when the weather keeps us shipbound. That is why the off-loading of the supply crates has made everyone more sociable. Last night after supper we sang together, led by Thomas Grinstead, our sailmaker, who played accordion. This began *before* the rum had been served.

I have thought about what the Captain said to me when he gave me this blank journal: "We are on the verge of solving the great mystery." Perhaps, if I concentrate on our purpose for being in this frozen land, I can lift my thoughts of the winter. If I can bring back the enthusiasm I felt eighteen months past, I hope my brooding will fade away.

This adventure began when I was twelve, in March, 1857. After my father's death, Rachel and I were sent to Weston-super-Mare to live with my Aunt Anne, my mother's sister, and her husband, Daniel Lockwood, a clothing merchant.

Money from my father's estate supported us, but it was still an act of great kindness for my aunt.

She had seven children of her own, and finding room for us in her house was a burden.

I was not the best-behaved child. Whenever I got into trouble, my uncle would want to take a cane to me, but my aunt had more patience. She would sit and talk to me, and from her I learned about my family.

I had always known that my father's sister, Jane, had married one of Great Britain's greatest heroes, Sir John Franklin. Their framed portraits were on our mantelpiece, and it always struck me how young my aunt looked compared to my uncle. Although my father wrote to his sister, there was never a suggestion that we might visit her. After all, Jane was a Lady.

So, it was a surprise when I received an invitation to visit the Franklin's London house in March of last year.

Shortly after my arrival, I was ushered into the library and my aunt introduced me to Francis McClintock. Lady Jane explained that McClintock, an Arctic explorer, was going to captain a private ship, the *Fox*, and sail her into Arctic waters. The purpose of the voyage was to finally discover the fate of my uncle, Sir John Franklin, and his crew, who have been missing for over a decade.

Captain McClintock asked me several questions — about my father, what I knew of Franklin's missing expedition and about the state of my health. He seemed pleased with my answers.

"Your aunt believes that you might wish to pursue a Navy career like your father," he said after a long conversation.

"It has always interested me, sir."

"Good. Well, I will need a ship's boy on board the *Fox*. Considering the quality of your background, your interest in the sea and your obvious robust health, I would like to offer you the position."

"Me?" I mumbled. "Go to the Arctic?"

"Don't stand there with your mouth open, boy. Would you like to sail with me? There will be hardships and danger. And you'll work for a living. Have no doubt about that. But there will be adventure as well. You'll be part of a crew that finally discovers what happened to your courageous uncle and the brave souls under his command."

"I'd be...delighted, sir." I was both stunned and excited. I had never imagined that I would be given such an opportunity.

My father had been on an earlier search for my uncle in 1850 on the *H.M.S Investigator*. Even though I was only six years old at the time, I can recall the day my father took me out to the garden and we sat on the stone bench.

"Peter," he began. "You know that your uncle, Sir John Franklin, is missing at sea. But do you really understand what has happened?"

I was anxious to show that I did. "I know that he is lost in the Ardic," I answered.

"Arctic," my father corrected. "In a few weeks, I will be going to search for Sir John. As I've told you, I won't see you for a year, perhaps two or three. But I want you to know that I am on a noble voyage. Let me tell you the tale and the great mystery that remains unanswered."

My father slowly stuffed tobacco into his clay pipe and took two long breaths before beginning. "In 1845, Sir John Franklin and one hundred twenty-eight other men set sail in two ships to complete the search for the passage through the Arctic Ocean on top of the Americas."

"It's cold there," I said.

He nodded. "Yes, very cold. So cold that the sea freezes for all but a few months. The sun vanishes in the autumn and doesn't return until the spring. Ships are stuck in the ice all winter."

"Why would my uncle want to go there?" I wondered.

My father thought about this question for a long time. "There are many reasons, Peter, and they are all worthy. Sir John Franklin was a hero. He was a man destined to achieve greatness. His voyage would complete the map of our world. It would bring honour to our Queen and our country. It was, in itself, an act of bravery. And it was a wonderful adventure — a story that could be shared by everyone in the civilized world."

"Is my uncle dead?"

"Perhaps," he nodded. "But perhaps he is still alive. We don't know. In 1845, Sir John and his company sailed on the *Erebus* and the *Terror*, two strong ships, with enough supplies to last for at least three years. He took the best food, preserved in cans. Your uncle had already voyaged to the north twice before. He knew the waters and the weather. The third expedition should not have failed. It could not have failed."

He paused and took another long draft of smoke. "But something went wrong. The trip that was supposed to take one year — two at the most — slipped into three. The Franklin Expedition didn't return. Everyone was amazed and puzzled. Where was he? Where were the ships? Many search

expeditions sent by the British Navy have found
nothing. It is as if one hundred twenty-nine souls,
and their ships, have vanished from the world."

He put his arm around my shoulders. "More
ships from Britain and America are journeying
north to try to discover their fate this summer. We
hope we will return with the answer to the mystery.
We owe Sir John and those men our full dedication.
They may still be alive, waiting for rescue. We must
never stop our quest to find out what happened."

My father did not solve the mystery. Over the
past ten years, thirty-nine expeditions have gone
to search out the fate of Sir John Franklin. Except
for the remains of a camp on Beechey Island where
the *Erebus* and the *Terror* spent their first winter,
nothing else was discovered. It was just as my
father told me so many years ago. The ships and
their crews seemed to have disappeared from the
Earth.

But there are other puzzles. At the Beechey
Island camp, there are three graves of crew
members who died aboard the *Erebus* and the
Terror that winter. What was the cause of their
deaths? On such a well-equipped voyage, three
deaths is a high number. And at the Beechey Island
camp is a pile of rusting, empty cans, far too many
to have actually been used. The seams on some of
these cans have split. Did part of the food supply
spoil? Did my uncle and his crew run out of food?

Three years ago, Dr. John Rae, who was
exploring the northern Arctic for the Hudson's Bay
Company, met some Inuit from King William
Island. These Natives told a story about a party of
Europeans dragging a boat on a sledge southward
across the ice in Victoria Strait. They told Rae that

they had found several corpses and that the Europeans had starved to death.

Those men were from the *Erebus* and the *Terror*. The Inuit had relics of the Franklin Expedition. Sir John's Order of Merit star and some silver spoons were traded.

How would the Inuit get such things if they had not found the wrecks of the two ships? If the Europeans dragging the sledges were abandoning the ships because they were starving, why would they bother to take silver spoons?

Rae's discovery was enough proof of disaster for the British Navy. Despite an outcry from the public, naval officials believed the Inuit stories and declared that all people on Sir John's voyage were dead.

For me it is proof of nothing. The questions have yet to be answered. I have not given up hope that my uncle is still alive. That is why I am here, frozen in a foreign sea.

That is why Captain McClintock is here, and the crew of the *Fox*. And that is why my aunt paid for our ship and her crew with her own money. We have taken up the search for survivors of the 1845 expedition.

If my father were alive, he would be proud that I'm a member of this expedition. He would be pleased that we're going to solve the mystery at last.

This is our plan: In late winter, Captain McClintock will take a sledge party down the coast of the Boothia Peninsula to try to make contact with the Inuit that Dr. Rae met. Then, in the spring, we will sledge to King William Island itself to search for the wrecks of the *Erebus* and the *Terror* and, we hope, the survivors.

If I concentrate on my purpose in enduring these hardships, then perhaps the winter will pass quickly. If I think that the mystery will be answered in a short time, if I remind myself how important our voyage is, then maybe the darkness will become less of a burden.

3

November 17, 1858. Aboard the Fox, *frozen in the ice off Port Kennedy, Bellot Strait.*

The wind has stopped, although the air remains damp, making it feel very cold. Today Lieutenant Hobson, the First Mate, and Mr. Young, the Second Mate, left the *Fox* with two sledge teams and dogs to set supply depots for the journey to find the King William Inuit. They will travel across Long Lake, which is north of us on Somerset Island, and then down the western coast of Boothia Peninsula. The lake runs parallel to Bellot Strait and, although it will take us several miles out of our way, its flat, frozen surface is the fastest route across the land. They should be away for about ten days, if the weather holds.

With so many of the crew absent, the Captain ordered me to scrub the walls and ceiling of the lower deck. Scrub them! Such is the wonderful life of the ship's boy.

When the Captain told me I would work for my living, I had no idea he was being so truthful. Work is too kind a word. Labour is better, even toil. I am butler, maid and servant to the officers. I wash their clothes, clean their rooms, make their beds and empty their toilet buckets. I open their canned food, help the cook prepare it and then serve and clear away their meals. I am up first in the morning with the cook to prepare their breakfast and last to sleep after serving their evening rum and turning down their beds. Between these duties, I am supposed to keep the second deck tidy and take care of the toilet buckets of the crew.

As well, I become helper to anyone who needs an extra pair of hands. So, especially when we're under sail and everyone is busy, I am apprentice to the stoker, the sailmaker and the quartermaster. When we're frozen in, I am less busy — a little less busy. But today I had to scrub!

"Did I hear a moan?" Captain McClintock asked after he gave the command. "Are you telling me that you resist my orders?"

"Sorry, sir. It's just such a hard job."

"But it's a job that the ship's boy does," the Captain pointed out.

"Yes, sir," I grumbled.

"Go on with you," the Captain said. "You complain too much."

That's easy for him to say. He doesn't have to do it.

Sometimes I get angry listening to the officers complain about how hard their life is. Seldom does a meal go by without one of them moaning about the sorry food they have to eat. *We* eat pemmican preserved in twenty-two pound cans — eleven pounds of meat, eleven pounds of grease — while the officers dine on individual cans of best beef packed in gravy. We eat salt pork. They eat their personal supplies of canned soups and jams.

The officers use candles for their light. On the lower deck, we burn fat lamps. Great blobs of ash constantly float through the air. The nauseating burnt-lard smell clings to our clothes. On days when the weather keeps us below deck, our faces and hair become coated with the lampblack. It is this greasy ash that I was ordered to clean from the lower deck.

It took great quantities of lye soap and scrubbing to remove the slimy residue from the wood of the ship. My hands are red, cracked and sore. I am only grateful that the off-loading gave me more room to work in.

The extra space on the lower deck has also permitted me to move my hammock closer to the stove. One of the other "privileges" of being ship's boy is that I must place my hammock farthest from the stove, in the coldest corner of the deck. Despite the packing of snow on the top deck and the canvas housing, the temperature on board never rises much higher than ten degrees above freezing. In my usual position, I sometimes have to sleep in my fur parka to keep warm. It's a treat to sleep in just my woollen underclothes.

After a full morning of scrubbing, the Captain allowed Anton and me to go hunting. We were hoping to find seals. Fresh seal steaks and liver would be a pleasant change. And the dogs have almost finished the seal meat that was shot in October.

Anton is an Inuit we hired a year ago in Upernavik, Greenland, to help care for our Arctic dogs. We've become close friends; he made my parka for me. He speaks the Inuit language and a little Danish, but no English.

Several of the crew tried to teach him our civilized tongue, but although he has learned a few words, he has great difficulty with sentences.

During the long frozen days in Baffin Bay last winter, I decided to try to learn the Northern speech. To my surprise, I have picked up his language so well that he seldom stumps me with a new word.

Everyone else finds this Inuit language extremely difficult. The throat sounds and clicks leave them tongue-tied. Even the Captain only knows a few phrases. Mr. Petersen jokes that I must be part Native.

Anton looks as if he is about sixteen, perhaps eighteen at the oldest. The Greenlanders don't bother to keep track of their years.

"I've lived through so many winters that I can't remember one from the other," Anton said to me in his Northern speech. " That means I'm old, no? Do you remember all your winters?"

"I guess I'm old, too," I agreed.

Today on our hunting trip, we walked several miles down the coast. The ice is now completely solid to the horizon. This time of year, it's usually easier to walk on the ice than the land. The snow becomes either solidly packed or blown free on the ice. On shore, we are often slowed by large drifts. Also, the ice reflects the moon and starlight, making it easier to see. On land, the rocks absorb this light.

Although there is no sun at all, our eyes have adjusted to the constant dimness. It's amazing how bright the deck lights are in the depth of winter. It's almost painful to work in their glare.

One good thing about winter hunting is that we no longer have to worry about stumbling on a curious bear. The creatures have moved to more southerly hunting grounds. The polar bears are the true kings of the North, bold animals that consider people as legitimate a dinner as a seal.

Although Anton says he's never seen a polar bear attack a person, last spring Thomas Grinstead had to fire at a bear that was stalking him. Unfortunately the bullet missed, but the *thwack* of the cartridge made the bear cautious enough to allow Grinstead to return to the safety of the *Fox*. And this autumn, Mr. Petersen noticed a large animal circling around him and luckily was able to kill it before it attacked.

Around mid-afternoon, Anton and I stopped to eat some salt meat. As usual, our hunt had been fruitless. We found a few frozen breathing holes, the holes that the seals keep open in the ice so they can suface for air, but nothing fresh. We haven't seen a live seal for weeks.

"Do you have a wife, Peter?" Anton asked.

"No," I answered. "Boys my age don't get married."

"What about girls your age. Do they have husbands?"

"Some, but most are a few years older."

He scratched at his wispy beard. "I had a wife once," he announced.

"I'm sorry," I said.

"You're sorry? About what?"

"I'm sorry about your wife. I'm sorry that she's dead," I explained.

"Dead? She's not dead. What makes you think she's dead?"

"You said that you *had* a wife. I thought that meant she was..."

He laughed loudly for several moments. "No, she's not dead. I let her other husband take her north to hunt reindeer."

"Her *other* husband?"

He nodded and licked the salt from his fingers.

"Your wife had two husbands?" I wondered.

"There weren't enough women," he explained. "A man needs a family, right? Sometimes there aren't enough men. Then we marry two or three wives. That makes sense, no?"

"I suppose..."

"What do you do in England if there are too many men. How do they find a family?"

"Well, I..."

I wondered what my Aunt Anne would think of Anton and I talking like this. I was sure she'd be shocked. And before I came to the North, I would have been a little surprised as well. No doubt I would have thought the practice of sharing a wife to be unusual — almost savage. But trying to survive in this wretched Arctic has shown me that although Great Britain is the greatest civilization ever to exist — the extent of our Empire proves that — in some circumstances Native cultures are the most practical.

"Do you have a woman...I mean, a girl, who you want to be your wife?" Anton asked.

"Not really."

"Either you do or you don't," he pointed out.

"Well, there is a cousin who is the daughter of my Aunt Anne."

"Tell me about this cousin."

"Her name's Elizabeth. We've been friends for a long time. I've lived with her family since my father died."

"And now she is your woman, no?"

"Well, I guess she's my...close friend," I agreed.

"Then you should be married," Anton announced.

"Your world and mine are very different," I smiled.

"But we are good friends, no?" He slapped the side of my parka.

"We're good friends, yes," I agreed.

We headed back to the ship. Again we failed to see any sign of a seal. But we discovered the remaining crew members in a heated game of rounders on the ice and quickly joined in.

Later, while getting the officers' supper, I discovered a full crate of Mr. Brand's jams. His other foodstuffs had been divided among the four officers. I asked Captain McClintock what I should do with these preserves. I was half hoping that he'd let me take them to the crew. After all, the officers have enough jellies to last for years. But the Captain told me to add them to Lieutenant Hobson's supplies.

"My First Mate has a generous sweet tooth. Let him enjoy the surplus," he declared.

So much for my wishful thoughts.

Before sleeping, I helped catch Puss, the ship's cat, so that Dr. Walker could force a mixture of seal oil and medicines down her throat. The cat has been ailing lately, hardly touching her food.

Fortunately, our cat is an excellent mouser. The *Fox* is completely free of rats and mice. Members of the crew who have been on previous Arctic voyages say that this is a wonderful blessing. They tell tales of rats so bold that the rodents actually crawled into their sleeping blankets to keep warm.

Mr. Petersen says that when he was on another expedition to search for Franklin in 1854, most of the crew was struck by scurvy and too ill to get out of their bunks. He said that the rats would climb onto these ailing sailors and start chewing on their flesh!

4

January 1, 1859. Aboard the Fox, *frozen in the ice off Port Kennedy, Bellot Strait.*

A brand new year, and the crew are still in holiday spirits. As I write this I can hear laughter from the galley and a mixture of pleasant dinner aromas that mask the stink of the lamps.

I have been lazy with this journal and make a New Year's resolution to try to be more faithful to these pages.

Besides my regular duties, I suppose one of the main reasons I haven't written more is because I've been studying in the evening. I think the Captain worries about the crew brooding, because he asked Dr. Walker to give us instruction. The doctor is teaching several of us about tides, mapping and navigation. In fact, Mr. Young has noted that I'm becoming so skilled in the use of charts and the compass that I would be a valuable asset aboard any Navy ship.

The extra study has kept me wonderfully occupied. Besides focusing on our quest, I now realize that constant activity, both physical and mental, is necessary to distract me from dwelling on the fact that we are frozen in the sea, an island of life in a land of emptiness.

Other activities are filling my time and providing excuses for not writing. I am helping to record the findings of the magnetic observatory on the shore. And I'm taking care of the dogs with Anton. We now have twenty-nine dogs, including five new puppies. Besides sharing his knowledge of the dogs, the Greenlander has taught me how to build a snow-hut. I don't think I would like to live in one of my poor buildings, but I think I might be able to survive a night.

Lieutenant Hobson and Mr. Young have completed the placing of supply depots for a late winter sledge trip to find the King William Inuit that Dr. Rae spoke to. The Captain has yet to inform us of the teams for the journey. But I hope that since Anton has taught me about handling the dogs and I can help our interpreter, Mr. Petersen, I will be one of the first considered.

We have now fully winterized the *Fox*. A storm last week gave us enough snow to complete our insulation. It took three days of shovelling, but there is now a foot-thick layer of packed snow on the top deck. And we've piled the snow up the sides of the ship from the ice to the gunwales. This has raised the inside temperature a few degrees.

On the few days when we have tolerable weather, I go hunting with Anton. We have been moderately successful — one hare and four ptarmigan, but still no seals. Mr. Petersen, who has now moved into Mr. Brand's cabin, shot two small reindeer, which has added variety to our menu. The Captain encourages the hunting. Not only does it provide fresh meat which helps prevent scurvy, but it gives the crew members who cannot read and write some occupation. Even sporting for non-edible game, such as owls and foxes, passes the time.

This morning, after I confessed to the Captain that it had been weeks since I last put pen to paper, he excused me from my ship's duties. "Consider it a well-deserved holiday," he said. "But I insist that you enter a passage in your journal."

"But I don't think that I have much to write about," I told him.

"When there's nothing to say, then describe the weather," he told me.

Here is a description of the weather: Terrible.

We have three choices: Cold and misty — so damp that the chill seeps through my woollies and parts of my body shrink and retreat. Or cold and windy — a wind that roars and whips the snow so viciously that no one can leave the *Fox* without risk to his life. Or cold and cold — so cold that even a short time on the deck causes such a searing pain in the throat and lungs that I can picture myself freezing from the inside out. On Christmas Day it was seventy-six degrees below freezing. The next day it was eighty degrees below freezing.

Last week, full of my fear of the cold, I asked Captain McClintock at what temperature air froze. He just laughed at me.

When I complained about the cold to Anton he told me that the weather sounded worse in England.

"Why do you say that?" I asked.

"Well, you told me it's foggy and it rains all the time."

"I didn't say *all* the time."

"Most of the time?"

"*Some* of the time," I corrected.

"Some? What does that mean? Ten days a year?"

"A little more."

"Twenty?"

"More."

"Thirty?"

"A little more."

"More? You said *some* of the time," Anton pointed out. "How many rainy, foggy days then? Fifty?"

"Maybe a hundred. And a few more, depending on the year."

He started to count on his fingers as if he was having trouble understanding the numbers. At last he shook his head in amazement. "That's most of a year, no?"

"It's not even a third of a year," I defended. "Not really."

He held a finger to his head as a comment on my sanity. "It's crazy to live in a place where it rains and makes fog so often."

"Well, I feel the same way about the cold," I told him.

"But at least it doesn't rain when it's cold." He smiled as if he had just won an important argument.

It has been taking me a long time to fall asleep. I think it's partly the holidays, but it's also excitement. The new year means that the sledge trips draw closer by the hour. 1859 is the year that we'll finally solve the Franklin mystery.

When I should be sleeping, I lie awake trying to picture the fate of my uncle and his crews. I see his two strong ships frozen in the ice. I see his tables stacked with the canned provisions and the fresh game they must have shot. I can imagine the hand-picked crew, the finest sailors in the world, sitting on their deck, drinking rum, smoking pipes, joking with each other. I imagine my uncle planning the route through the islands during break-up.

And I wonder what went wrong.

What on earth and under heaven could have happened to them?

It just doesn't make any sense at all. There was a mere few hundred miles of Arctic sea left uncharted. It was so well planned — the men so experienced.

Because of the cans on Beechey Island, some people believe that everyone starved to death. Newspaper writers point to those cans as proof that they ran out of food.

But if they were running out of food, if the canned goods were rotten, my uncle would have turned his ships around and returned to England for fresh supplies. They left Beechey Island in 1846 to complete their quest. They must have believed they had enough food to last.

And then there's always fresh game. Look at Dr. Kane's search voyage of a few years ago. He survived a whole winter on what he hunted. Mr. Petersen was on that voyage. Although it was tough and scurvy threatened their fate, they survived. The Franklin Expedition would have hunted in the same way.

Other people think that scurvy might have overtaken them. But the disease takes time to develop. It's caused by poor food and lack of exercise. I cannot imagine my uncle allowing that to happen. Fresh game would help prevent the disease. Besides, scurvy afflicts some seriously and others barely at all. If scurvy was a problem, they would have returned home.

A storm? Captain McClintock says that serious gales in these islands, where there is little open sea, aren't a threat during the sailing season. "Ice is more of a problem," he told me. "The ice can crush a ship or beach it."

Suppose that did happen? Even if the ships were destroyed by the pack ice, it wouldn't have been sudden. The crews would have made it to land. The relics from Dr. Rae's Inuit suggest that the Natives boarded a deserted ship. How could they have got silver spoons otherwise? Starving, scurvy-ridden crew would not have bothered with silver cutlery.

That means that the ships were abandoned. But why? Why were they dragging a boat across the ice to the south? Why did they vanish? Why?

Only the thought that I will know the answers very soon finally allows me to sleep.

5

January 2, 1859. Aboard the Fox, *frozen in the ice off Port Kennedy, Bellot Strait.*

The holidays are officially over. After breakfast, Captain McClintock asked me to take down all the flags and banners that the crew had draped on the lower deck as our Christmas decorations. There's a certain sadness in seeing the *Fox* in her usual dress.

On Christmas Day, we invited the officers to the lower deck. The party was full of singing and laughter. The officers contributed a large cheese and some preserves to our meal. And a true feast it was. The mess tables were covered like the counter of a bake shop. We served ptarmigan, hare, hams and meat pies. Our breads ranged from sweet loaves to puffs. And for afters we had a choice of apple tarts, gooseberry pies and plum pudding. Everyone drank their rum in wine glasses. As you may guess, I went to bed with a full and somewhat uncomfortable stomach.

The Captain topped the celebration by giving us a gift of candles for our Christmas Box. It was a pleasant relief from the lamps.

Yesterday we had a similar party for the New Year, although the food wasn't quite as fancy. Once again the officers visited our deck and the Captain spoke to the whole crew. He offered thanks for our good fortune over the past year. "Let us remember how close we came to perishing in the pack ice last spring. Let us give thanks to our Lord for His intervention."

How well I remember that day, April 23, 1857....

After being frozen in Baffin Bay for six months, we'd spent two weeks in new ice. Several times the ship had broken loose from this new ice and made sail, but was forced back into the pack. That Saturday morning, the ice began to break apart quickly when we encountered an ocean swell.

As the swell increased, it broke the large pieces of ice into chunks. By nightfall, the pieces were smaller than the *Fox*. These crashed into each other with incredible violence. They also bounced against our tiny ship.

I tried to bunk down at about ten o'clock, but the noise of ice smashing against the hull so frightened me that I got dressed again and headed for the top deck.

When I climbed through the hatchway, I checked on the dogs. They were curled by the midmast, most of them sleeping despite the heaving of the ship. A couple of huskies raised their heads as I approached.

Captain McClintock was overlooking the stern, watching the dark ice thud and bump in the black water.

I shuffled carefully, trying to balance my movement with the sway of the ship.

"It isn't good, is it, sir?" I asked as I grabbed a sailrope on the sternmast.

The Captain didn't answer.

"We're in trouble, aren't we, sir?" I said more loudly.

He turned to me as two masses of ice collided and shot spray over us.

"Peter?" the Captain wiped salt water from his eyes. "What are you doing on deck?"

"I can't sleep," I told him. "The noise of the ice crashing against the hull sounds like the inside of a drum."

"The deck is no place for the boy when the sea is like..."

The screech of grating ice drowned out his words.

"I don't want to stay under," I protested. "If something is going to happen, I want to be here."

Captain McClintock nodded as if my request was reasonable. I shivered at that. Then he made a tight smile and patted my shoulder a few times. "We'll be all right, Peter."

"What's happening?" I asked.

He pointed at the churning water. "It's just what you see, boy. We're on the edge of the pack now. And the sea is welcoming us with anger. The edge of the ice is always dangerous." Then he pointed to the flag on the mainmast. "But to make it worse, the wind has shifted to the south-west. It may bring a gale."

I sensed the wind. It wasn't that strong. And we'd survived a fierce gale as we rounded Greenland the previous summer. The *Fox* could handle a rough sea.

"We can ride a storm," I said.

"But not the ice," the Captain frowned. "If the swells increase, then the ice will be hurled against us. The waves will blast the chunks right through the hull. We won't stand a chance."

A small piece rubbed across our port side and sent a ribbon of spray into the air.

"It's five feet now," the Captain declared. "If the swell gets any higher, the ice will batter the *Fox* into matchsticks."

By midnight, the waves were cresting eight feet above the trough. The *Fox* rose and splashed in the boiling water. Ice thudded and scraped the ship. Fortunately, the larger pieces drifted by us. But it was obvious that our luck would not hold out much longer.

The Captain maintained his watch of the sea, speaking only to the helmsman. I stayed on deck, despite the fact that my parka was soaked and the water had seeped through to my skin. Members of the crew would poke their heads from the hatchway, look around for a few moments, and then return to the lower levels.

"Steer straight into the swell!" the Captain shouted suddenly. "Due course!"

The ship shifted a few degrees to starboard and the waves exploded against the bow. I heard the whine of the propeller as the stern rose from the water. Two large chunks of pack ice lifted with a wave and fell away from us.

"You really should be below, Peter," the Captain said.

I stayed where I was, holding the rope and watching the chaos of Baffin Bay.

"The sea spirits are angry. They have come to claim us."

I twisted around to see Anton holding another rope and staring into the sea. Then he looked at me.

There were wide circles of white around his brown eyes. "I'm scared," he said. "I am too young to go to the land of the dead."

A wave brought a spray of water that broke over the dogs. A few of them stirred and howled in protest.

"Are we going to die?" Anton asked.

A couple of the dogs began to bark.

"Keep the dogs quiet," the Captain ordered. "Anton, take care of the dogs."

Anton glanced at the Captain and I translated the order. He nodded and seemed to take strength from the command as he moved toward the dogs.

The wind gusted, throwing the swells well over ten feet. The Captain yelled angry words at the sea. Behind me, I heard two crew members praying.

"Peter!" the Captain ordered. "Come here!"

I released the rope and stumbled to the stern. "Aye, sir?" I said.

He looked at me with the same jerking eyes he was using to watch the ice. "Go below and get my Bible."

"Your Bible?"

"The time has..." Ice deflected off the bow. Water washed the entire deck. "Get my Bible."

I saluted and fumbled to the hatchway. I tripped on the steep stairs and slid to the officers' deck.

I grabbed the Bible from the Captain's bookshelf, scrambled back up the hatchway and handed the book to Captain McClintock.

"This is a good time to ask for a miracle, Peter," he said.

A large chunk of ice humped at the port side. The *Fox* tilted at a sharp angle for a moment and then straightened with a jerk.

"Get me a lantern," the Captain ordered.

I unhooked an oil lamp from the mast and held it over his shoulder as he flipped the pages. I noticed that many of the crew were now on deck. They crowded around the stern.

"Gentlemen," the Captain acknowledged their presence. "Let us seek the help of our creator. I read from the forty-sixth psalm: 'God is our refuge and strength, a very present help in trouble. Therefore will not we fear, though the earth be removed, and though the mountains be carried into the midst of the sea; Though the waters therefore roar and be troubled...'"

A crash of ice sent a shower of spray over us. The *Fox* shivered as another large mass thumped off the port bow.

If a chunk hit us right on...

In the gloom of the ocean I caught sight of a small iceberg, about sixty-five feet high. "Berg!" I interrupted.

The Captain snapped his head up from the Bible and saw the dark silhouette in the dark ocean. "Hard starboard!" he called to the helmsman.

I watched the swirling sea throw vicious waves at the face of the iceberg. The showers rose as high as the summit. And then I saw the calm water.

"Wait!" I shouted. "Look!" I pointed at the back of the iceberg. "Behind the ice!"

The berg was ploughing through the pack chunks, making a channel of calm water. Instead of churning, the sea swirled in eddies.

The Captain searched the darkness. "By heaven!" Then he laughed. "Port, helmsman. Get this ship in the lee of the berg."

Our tiny vessel pulled left and bumped into a large mass. The hull timbers creaked and groaned. For a moment I wondered if we would be ripped apart a short distance from our potential salvation.

But the *Fox* eased into the calm of the berg. Suddenly the swaying and rocking settled into a more normal swell. And just as suddenly, there was a shout from someone on deck.

"Three cheers for the boy! Hip, hip..."

"Hooray!" the crew shouted.

The Captain smiled at me as the ship's company cheered. "Your sharp eyes may have saved our souls, Peter."

I smiled stupidly. "But I..."

"Helmsman," the Captain called, "you and I will remain on deck and make sure that we follow this berg until we reach open sea. But for everyone else, break out Allsop's ale."

Captain McClintock pulled at my wet parka. "Go and dry off," he said. "And enjoy the good ale before you bunk down."

I shook my head. "With your permission, sir, I'd like to remain on deck."

The Captain winked at Lieutenant Hobson. "I think we've found someone looking for your job."

The crew broke into hearty laughter and then, enjoying our new-found calm, headed below to drink the Captain's gift.

How long ago that seems. To think that the *Fox* actually floated in the sea. It seems as if we have been frozen here for eternity.

6

January 4, 1859. Aboard the Fox, *frozen in the ice off Port Kennedy, Bellot Strait.*

Stomach pains sent me to see Dr. Walker yesterday.

"How long have you had them?" he asked.

"Three days, but they only started to hurt badly today."

"And when did you last move your bowels?" he asked.

"A week. Ten days."

"Then I have a good idea what's wrong," he nodded. "You need a purge."

"Oh, no," I groaned.

Slow bowels are a constant curse for everyone on board. It must have something to do with our diet. But I'm not sure which is worse, the constipation or Dr. Walker's cure. He pours a vile green liquid down our throats and promises "a speedy completion to your digestion."

I spent most of this morning squatting over a bucket on the top deck. The cramps were almost unbearable. It was at least minus 30 under the canvas housing, yet at the same time I was freezing my buttocks, my face was sweating.

I do feel much better than I have in a week, though, and enjoyed a full meal at supper.

After the issue of rum this evening, the Captain wished to talk to the officers in private, so instead of serving them, I was able to join the crew in their after-meal conversation.

Although I am starting to tolerate, if not enjoy, the taste of rum, I am still a long way from being able to drain my daily allowance. And I don't think I'll ever be able to down it as quickly as some of the crew.

After the rum was passed around, many of the crew lit their pipes. The conversation quickly turned to talk about their wives or sweethearts. Everyone told how they first met their ladies, and the married crewmates described their weddings and their homes. Needless to say, there were several damp eyes during their descriptions.

Only Thomas Blackwell, one of the ship's stewards, refused to share the stories. Lately he has been withdrawn and brooding. Perhaps the darkness is weighing on him. Or it could be his diet. I have noticed that he never eats the fresh game we kill. He just eats the canned meat.

When Thomas Grinstead had finished telling us about his wife, all eyes turned to the next person. Me.

After it dawned on me that they were waiting for my story, I shook my head. "I have nothing to say. I don't have a sweetheart."

"Then you must have a wife," someone joked.

"I was only twelve when we left Aberdeen," I pointed out.

"When I was twelve, I had this many sweethearts." Thomas Grinstead held up all his fingers.

There was much laughter, and Grinstead slapped me on the shoulder. "Not even one, Peter?"

"Well," I said. "There is Elizabeth."

"Ah," someone clapped. "There *is* Elizabeth."

"What is she like?" Grinstead asked.

"Well, she's...her hair is like a flaming mane, all red and copper and waving down her back. And her eyes sparkle, a brilliant green, alight with laughter. And the way she does laugh. It's almost like music. When I hear it it makes me..." I stopped and looked at the men staring at me. I felt my face flush. "I'm sorry, I didn't mean..."

"Sorry?" Grinstead said softly. "Don't be sorry."

"To be young and in love," someone said.

"Think of how much more beautiful she'll be when you see her this summer," Grinstead told me.

Lately she's been on my mind a good deal.

I can remember the first time I understood that she liked me in a special way. I was just turned eleven. She was ten. I was helping in my Aunt Anne's garden and she was resting from her kitchen chores.

It was May, lots of blossoms and flowers. The weather had been sunny for several days and Elizabeth's cheeks had turned as red as her hair.

"Hello, Peter," she smiled. "What are you doing?"

I held up my left hand to show her several bloody wounds in my fingers. "Rose thorns," I told her. "I'm trimming the rose bushes and I'm having an awful time."

She laughed.

"You want to see me pass out?" I asked.

"Pardon?"

"You want to see me faint?"

"Why would I want to see you faint?" she wondered. "Besides, nobody can just faint when they want to."

"I can," I bragged. "If you help me. John Simmons showed me how yesterday when I was in his father's shop."

"I have to help you?"

"Right. Then I'll faint."

"How?"

I turned around so my back was facing her.

"Put your arms around me. Just at the bottom of my ribs."

She slipped her arms around my waist and clamped her hands over my stomach.

"A little higher," I coached. "And not so tight. Not yet, anyway."

"What am I supposed to do? How is this going to make you faint?" she asked.

"You'll see. I'm going to take ten deep breaths. After I breathe out the tenth time, you squeeze as hard as you can."

"Then you'll pass out?"

"Out cold," I insisted.

"You won't just be pretending?"

"Of course not."

"I don't believe it."

"Just do it," I said. "Start counting my breaths."

I sucked in a deep breath and blew it out slowly.

"One," Elizabeth counted.

I sucked in another deep breath.

By the time Elizabeth said "Nine," my head was already floating and the blossoms were beginning to dance in little circles.

I drew in the last lungful of air and pushed it from my chest. Elizabeth squeezed at the same time. Hard. With more strength than I thought she owned. As the vise tightened around my ribs, the blossoms turned into grey stars. I tried to suck in a breath, but Elizabeth's arms stopped me. The grey stars twinkled on a purple background for a moment, and then I fainted.

I'm not sure how long it took before the black turned to purple and then to light, but when I came to, I saw Elizabeth's face barely inches from mine. She looked so serious and so concerned that I began to laugh.

She punched my chest. "Peter Griffin!" she scolded. "I was really worried about you. Your eyes were rolled up into your head. It was terrible." She punched my chest again. "How could you scare me like that?"

"You looked so funny," I laughed.

She pounded my ribs for a third time. "I'll never speak to you ever again." She walked away with her back straight, her head thrown back and her red hair bouncing with each angry step. It was at that moment that I knew she liked me. And I knew I felt the same way about her.

What I would do for a letter from Elizabeth.

7

January 26, 1859. Aboard the Fox, *frozen in the ice off Port Kennedy, Bellot Strait.*

A few weeks between my journal entries. As last time, I've been busy doing little things — chores, dogs and navigation lessons. But three things happened today that are worth recording.

First, just after midday meal, a half disk of sun rose above the horizon for a few moments. Although it doesn't bring any warmth, and only a little more brightness to the daytime twilight, it does wonders for my spirits. Each day will now take us a step away from the cold and dark. We will be in deep winter for another three months, and the ice break-up is still a half year away, but the returning sun tells us that we are moving toward summer rather than slipping away from it.

Second, the return of the light means that we can begin our final preparations for the sledge trips to find the King William Inuit.

The Captain will lead a team across Long Lake, north of Bellot Strait, and down the western coast of Boothia Peninsula. As I have written, the Captain hopes to travel to the winter village of the Inuit Rae met five years ago. If these Natives can be found, then information about the wrecks of the *Erebus* and the *Terror* may be discovered. Then we will know exactly where to travel on the spring sledge journeys.

And I am going! Just as I had hoped, Captain McClintock selected me as a member of this important team.

This afternoon, as I was serving his tea and scones, he asked me to stay for a few moments.

"Peter," he said. "I'm just making the last of the arrangements for the three-week sledge trip down Boothia."

"Yes, sir. The sun returned today. There'll soon be enough light for travelling."

"I plan to set out on the morning of February 15th."

"May God speed and protect you," I said.

He nodded. "I've been thinking about who should accompany me."

"Yes, sir?"

"I am going to take Mr. Petersen. He is, of course, expert in the Northern language. And Anton, the Greenlander, to help care for the dogs."

"Those are good choices, sir."

"And I also plan to take Alexander Thompson, the quartermaster. He's a big man and I will need his strength."

Then the Captain leaned back in his chair and stared at me under his eyebrows. "And I've decided to take along Peter Griffin. He, too, is strong. And he knows the Native tongue and how to handle dogs. And, as I noticed a while ago, he can build a snow hut."

It was difficult to stop the smile stretching across my face. "Thank you, sir. Nothing could make me happpier."

"It's not an act of charity, Peter," he said soberly. "I'm taking you because I feel you will be useful."

"Thank you, sir." I continued to smile.

Indeed, I was so excited, I was lightheaded. We are so close to solving the mystery that so many have tried to answer. An entire nation, no, the entire Empire is anxiously waiting for what we will discover.

The third event was a surprise gift from the officers.

"One more thing before you go," the Captain said.

"Yes, sir?"

He reached into his desk drawer and took out a small, rectangular box. "The officers would like to acknowledge your service over the past year with a small token. A gift."

"A gift?"

"We guessed that you probably didn't pack one of these when you left Aberdeen, and we've noticed that you're in need of one at present."

I opened the lid, unwrapped the tissue paper and discovered a fine razor inside. The blade was Sheffield steel and the handle was mother of pearl.

"Thank you, sir. Thank you most kindly."

"You have the beginnings of an excellent moustache," the Captain said. "But right now it looks untidy, as if you have a dirty face. In order to thicken it up, you have to shave it."

"Yes, sir."

"Well, what are you waiting for?"

When I went below deck and showed my gift to the crew, they began to applaud.

"I suppose this means we can't call you 'the boy' anymore," Thomas Grinstead joked.

44

Since Grinstead has grown a beard this winter, he loaned me his shaving brush, mug and soap. With the crew as an audience, I lathered up and removed the fuzz. Everyone cheered my clean face despite the two cuts I gave myself.

"Things must be fairly boring if my first shave is so entertaining," I said to Grinstead.

"A man only has his first shave once," he told me. "Congratulations, Peter. You know, we wait so long for the whiskers to come and then we spend the rest of our lives shaving them off or scratching them in a itchy beard. You can borrow my kit when you need another shave. Next month." Then he started to laugh.

8

February 1, 1859. Aboard the Fox, *frozen in the ice off Port Kennedy, Bellot Strait.*

Today on our hunting trip, Anton and I passed the grave of George Brand.

"You know, Peter," Anton said, pointing at the tombstone, "I've thought about this grave many times. I've wondered why you spent all those days digging it."

"Because the ground was frozen," I told him.

"If the ground is frozen, then it is foolish to dig, no? Digging into the ground to bury your dead is so like you."

"Like me?"

"Like your people," he corrected. "You walk out of step with the world."

"Hardly," I laughed. "Our search for the northern passage between the oceans is the last part of the world's shoreline to be mapped. We've been everywhere else."

"But you don't seem to have learned anything from where you've been."

"The sun never sets on the British Empire," I defended.

"The sun never sets on Greenland in the summer," he countered.

"That's not what I mean," I told him. "Britain has control of many lands all over the world. Somewhere it's always daytime on British territory."

"Then tell me how people who claim to be so great can spend so much time chipping at frozen ground to make a hole big enough for a body?"

"It's the right thing to do. It shows respect."

"But doesn't dressing a body in fine skins and placing it in a hollow also show respect? And doesn't it leave more time for important things like hunting and eating and — "

I didn't let him finish. "For your people. We're different."

He nodded slowly. "There is so much that is different. Even your feeling about names is different. Take your name. What does Peter mean?"

"It's just a name."

"So it means nothing," he asserted. "It is *just* a name and you are *just* a person. You are more than that, no? You have a living spirit."

"What does Anton mean?" I asked.

"Nothing," he told me. "It is the name the Danish gave me. They, too, use names with no meaning. My Inuit name is Auglituk. It means 'one with the joyful cry.' Anton is just a name. Auglituk is the sound of a spirit. Do you see the difference?"

"It doesn't seem all that important."

"But it is. It is. Your people cannot hear the songs of the spirits."

"You mean our religion? We're very true to our God," I said. "Don't we have chapel every Sunday? And grace before meals? And you've seen me read my Bible. I do it most days."

"The Danes in Greenland have taught me about your God. And I see you pray to Him. You hope He listens to you, but you don't try to listen to His songs on the breeze."

"What are you talking about?"

"You fight against His songs."

"Hold on." I held up my hands. "I don't understand. I don't fight any songs — whatever that means."

"Burying a body because it is your way fights a song of this land. The land says there are other ways."

"But not *our* way...." I paused and tried to organize my thoughts.

"Exactly." Anton nodded.

"But..."

"You're deaf to the sounds. Do you want more proof? Who else, but one who cannot hear the spirits, kills for no reason? Why do your people kill everything with your guns? Why do you kill things that you don't eat? What joy is there in killing an owl?"

"It's..." I tried to find an Inuit word for sport. "It's a game. It's for fun."

"It's fun to kill for no reason?"

"I...look, Anton. They're just animals."

"And you don't believe that animals have souls?"

"Of course they don't."

My friend glanced out across the frozen sea. "Whenever I kill something, do you know what I do?"

"You pray. I've watched you," I answered. "You thank God for the kill."

He shook his head. "I pray. But you're wrong about who I thank. I thank the animal I've just killed. I thank the seal for giving up its life so that I can live."

"It didn't have much choice, did it?" I smiled. "You stuck a spear into it."

Anton didn't return the smile. Instead he pointed at his ears. "Deaf," he said. "Your people frighten me, Peter. What will happen on the day when you kill everything? One day you'll find that there is nothing left. Just you and all the holes you've dug."

"You don't know how big the world is. There's so much. Enough to last forever."

"Look at this land and tell me how much of everything there is."

"You're being foolish, Anton," I said. "When we get back to the ship, I'll show you books that tell of other places. Warm places where there are — "

"No," he interrupted. "A deaf person cannot whistle the song he doesn't hear."

Tonight I asked Dr. Walker about the grave and why the Captain ordered it dug.

"A strange question," he said. "What else should he have done? We have to bury our dead."

"Couldn't we have chopped through the ice and buried Brand at sea, like we did Robert Scott?" I suggested.

Dr. Walker frowned. "What are you thinking, boy? The ship was anchored. Captain McClintock is a Navy man and Navy regulations dictate a shore burial, if at all possible."

"But it took so long to dig the frozen ground."

"Four days," the doctor pointed out. "What if it took a week, a month, two months? What else does the crew have to do all winter? You're acting peculiar, Peter."

"It's just that I was talking to Anton, and he was saying..."

"He was saying what? No, I don't want to hear it. You shouldn't listen to claptrap, my boy. You start listening to the Native superstitions and you end up asking those stupid questions. Remember who you are. You're British."

"Yes, sir," I nodded.

"Good. Now go have a mug of ale."

"Yes, sir."

"Go celebrate with Robert Hampton. Do you know he shot a fox pup today?"

"What did he do with it?"

"Do with it?" the doctor asked. "It was just a pup. It was far too small for a decent pelt. He left it. Why do you ask?"

"No reason," I said.

9

February 16, 1859. Aboard the Fox, *frozen in the ice off Port Kennedy, Bellot Strait.*

A storm has been blowing for the last three days. But the winds died this evening and we're leaving tomorrow morning.

It's well after midnight and I am sitting at a mess-table writing by oil lamp. Thomas Grinstead complained about my light, but I think he's asleep now. I know that it would be useless for me to try to use my hammock. My excitement is too great. I'd just toss and turn until breakfast.

What will it be like in the middle of this Arctic land, deep in winter, miles from the safety of the ship? I find my thoughts wandering to scenes of disaster. I see myself lost from the sledge, stumbling through the cold darkness, fingers and toes black from frostbite, feeling the air suck my life as it steals my warmth.

And what will we discover when we finally meet the Inuit? Will we find the answers we have been searching for? I've decided to take my journal with me to record the events of our journey.

Thomas Blackwell doesn't seem to be getting any better. He's been complaining of backaches and stiffness. Dr. Walker has ordered him to get more exercise and to eat more fresh game.

What else can I write to waste the Captain's ink? Oh, yes, a nasty story that shows the savage nature of the Inuit dogs. Last week, Anton had to muzzle one of the dogs overnight. My friend was getting the team used to sleeping in harness and this particular animal spent a good deal of her time trying to chew through the leather.

When Anton and I went to check on the animals before breakfast the next day, we found the dog lying in a mess of blood. She was still alive, but just barely. The other dogs had attacked her during the night and simply chewed her to pieces. Muzzled, she couldn't defend herself. A truly horrible death. What savage creatures they are!

The dogs are valuable to us, but I certainly don't have much affection for them. When I first watched Anton beat and whip them, I thought that he was treating them cruelly. Now I realize it's the only way to gain their respect.

Mr. Petersen tells a story of the time he was on Dr. Kane's Expedition to find my uncle in 1854. On a sledge trip, one of his dogs broke free of the harness during the evening and ate part of the supply of walrus meat. Petersen was so angry that he beat the dog on the head with a piece of wood. "Thrashed it soundly. Tried to beat its brains out," is the way he describes it. "Next morning the animal was pulling the sledge as if nothing had happened."

Truly savage beasts.

What else? The comet. Three nights ago I was emptying the toilet buckets before bed, when I noticed the streak in the sky.

Anton was tending to the dogs and I called to him. "Look!" I pointed at the comet that was below the Great Bear constellation.

"A star with the tail of a seal," he noted.

"It's a comet."

"A comet?"

"I saw one when I was younger. They're something like planets, but different."

"Like planets?"

"You know, the stars that move. I'll explain later. But that's a comet. Its tail always faces away from the sun. This is really exciting."

When I told Dr. Walker about it, he climbed on deck, looked at the comet, and charged below again to get his measuring instruments. When he returned and set them up, Anton stared at him with great curiosity.

"What is he doing, Peter?"

"He's going to find the path of the comet."

"How can he do that?"

"It's going around the sun," I explained. "The doctor is trying to map its journey."

"I'll record the time and date you spotted this," Dr. Walker told me. "When we return, we'll check with the Royal Observatory in London. There is a small chance that you may have been the first person to see it. If that's the case, the comet will be named after you."

"Do you mean it?"

"A small chance," the doctor nodded. "Who knows? One day people may look up and say, 'There is Griffin's Comet.'"

Anton asked me what the doctor was saying. When I translated, he looked even more puzzled. "Why would a comet want your name?"

"Tomorrow we'll look in the books," I told him. "I'll tell you about the sky."

Anton and I have spent many hours examining the books. After I tried to explain about the moon, planets and stars, I think he is completely confused. He keeps looking into the sky as if he's trying to figure out something terribly difficult.

I feel the same way about our strange talk about being deaf to the sound of the spirits. The other day Mr. Petersen returned with an owl he'd shot and an ermine he'd trapped. True, Dr. Walker sketched both animals, and Petersen kept the ermine's pelt. But it does seem a waste in a way.

I suppose I'm just seeing the Inuit's limited view of nature. In the Arctic, there is so little. Everything is valuable. I wish I could explain to him how truly large our planet is. How killing a few animals means nothing. There are so many more.

A most unusual thing happened yesterday. I was opening a large cask of biscuit for the cook and found a mouse inside! This was more than a little surprise, since there are no mice on the ship. Puss killed the last a few days out of Aberdeen.

Although the mouse was small, it was mature. The biscuit cask was packed watertight in Aberdeen and there was no hole for the mouse to enter. This means that the mouse has lived inside all this time.

"At least it proves one thing," the Captain said. "It shows us how nutritious our biscuit is."

Nutritious, maybe, but I surely wish it tasted a little better.

"Kill that bloody light or I'll box your bloody ears!" Thomas Grinstead has just threatened me.

I suppose I now have to toss and turn.

10

February 22, 1859. Camped on the western coast of Boothia Peninsula, approximately 50 miles south of Bellot Strait.

A storm prevents us from travelling today. Although everyone is disappointed, the Captain pointed out, "We've made good distance. The delay will rest the dogs and heal their feet."

It also gives me a chance to write in my journal. I've thawed some ink on the cooking stove, but I am not sure how long I'll be able to write before I have to put on my mittens to warm my hands.

We set out five days ago and directed the sledges across Long Lake that runs parallel to Bellot Strait. We made good speed on the ice. In fact, we reached the west coast that evening. Our snow hut was built near Pemmican Rock.

The next day we began our journey southward. The weather was bitter — a strong Northwest wind at our backs with the thermometer stuck at minus 48. The third day wasn't any better. The hard snow and ice must hurt the dogs' feet, because several of them act lame and a couple have repeatedly fallen into fits. We've dropped some of our provisions to lighten their load.

I've just had to stop writing for several minutes to thaw my fingers. It seems that I have about ten minutes of writing time between warm-ups.

The cold has produced a hardship that Petersen and Captain McClintock find especially annoying. It has turned the rum as thick as molasses.

When I tried to pour the Captain a draft from the cask, it oozed out as thick glump.

"What's happened to our grog?" Petersen moaned.

The Captain handed his cup back to me. "From now on, thaw it first, Peter."

I have to heat the rum the same way I do the ink. I think that part of the spirit must boil away because everyone complains that the liquid has lost its "bite."

So far, our journey has followed this routine. We break camp before sunrise, with the Captain leading the way. Petersen and Thompson drive the dogs and follow close behind. Anton walks behind Petersen and I stay on the heels of Thompson. When they become tired, we take over the dogs and they follow us.

When we break for the evening, Captain McClintock, Thompson and Anton saw the compressed snow into blocks. Then they bring it to Petersen and myself. We build the snow hut.

In the interest of speed, we don't dome the roof in the Inuit manner. Instead we build it tall and slope it slightly inward. Once we have a height of about five feet, we throw the tent over the top to make a roof.

After the hut is finished, Anton and I feed the dogs. This is a difficult chore because the animals are so hungry and vicious that they fight over the meat. We have to make sure that the weaker dogs get their share.

During this time, Thompson and Petersen carry our gear into the hut. The Captain sets up the stove and arranges our sleeping bags, made of doubled blankets.

When Anton and I are finished, the door is sealed, the stove lit and dinner prepared. Then the men smoke their pipes and drink rum.

As soon as the stove is extinguished, the temperature in the hut falls rapidly. It's impossible to drink our tea without wearing our mittens. We then snuggle into our blankets, pull the hoods over our heads and hope the feeble sleeping bags keep out the cold.

The constant activity has given me little chance to think about the danger of our trek. Our lives are in the hands of a small stove, a small supply of food and our health. If the weather turned foul for a week, if we injured ourselves or fell ill, we would be in serious trouble in a short time.

I mustn't write this. Writing about it spurs my imagination. I must concentrate on our purpose.

For the last two nights, my dreams have been of summer. I'm visiting the beach in Weston-super-Mare, enjoying the warm breeze from the sea. The sand is hot, too hot to walk on. Elizabeth and I are running across it, so we can wade in the tide.

How different the dreams are to reality.

11

March 1, 1859. Camped on the western coast of Boothia Peninsula, near the Magnetic North Pole.

It's two hours before midnight and everyone is asleep. Anton fell into deep snoring about ten minutes ago. I have managed to melt some ink using the sole oil lamp that illuminates our excellent snow hut.

The roof of our house is shaped of large, curving blocks of snow. The heat from our cooking stove and bodies has glazed the interior to a smooth shine. It offers excellent insulation. The temperature feels a few degrees above the freezing mark, warm enough to write without my mitts.

The reason we are sleeping in such a well-built house this evening is that *we* didn't build it. Right now, I'm looking at four Inuit hunters we met today. They sleep in their parkas, sitting on the snow floor, leaning against one of the walls, with their heads on their chests. These four hunters built the hut for us. In return for their labour, the Captain gave each of them a needle.

We had just stopped to camp for the evening at a point Captain McClintock said is near the Magnetic North Pole. No sooner had we chosen the best spot to build the hut, than we saw four Inuit with their dogs approaching us.

After the Captain and Petersen greeted them, they told us that they had been seal hunting on the ice. Petersen declared that we wished to barter with them and showed them the things that we had to trade — files, knives, beads, scissors, needles and so on. Of course, they were most interested.

This much we have found out:

One of the hunters was wearing a Navy button on his coat. He said it came from some starved Europeans on a island near a river where there are salmon. Then he showed us his knife. It had been fashioned from a piece of iron. The hunter said he got the metal at the same place.

Another of the Natives told us that he had met Dr. Rae and his party.

Hardly terrific news. But tomorrow they promised to bring their whole village to meet us. We should be able to find somebody who can tell us some useful information.

Right now, I'm holding the button. It's not unusual, just a common brass stud with an anchor stamped on it. But it was worn on the greatcoat of someone from the Franklin Expedition, and that makes it special.

I have heard about my uncle's voyage all of my life, puzzled over it, wondered about it, dreamed of it. For almost two years, I've lived in this miserable environment to get close to the frozen part of the globe where those men vanished. All that time, it has existed only in my mind. But now, with this small button, I finally have something that physically belonged to the expedition. It makes it real, my purpose in being here all the more important.

Tomorrow we meet with Natives who may have been aboard the *Erebus* and the *Terror*. Wouldn't it be wonderful if we discover the place where survivors are waiting for our rescue?

Oh, I wish this little brass stud could tell me its story. I wish it would answer all of my questions right now — tell me the fate of its owner.

It was interesting to watch Petersen interview the Inuit. At one point I was puzzled by his questions, and only later understood what he was doing.

"You have a warm winter?" Petersen asked one of the hunters. "Good fires?"

The Inuit smiled and nodded.

"No wood," another hunter snapped. "He doesn't mean wood."

"You have wood?" Petersen asked the first man.

"He doesn't mean wood," the second hunter protested. "Warm fires don't mean wood."

"Talk to them one at a time," the Captain ordered.

After Petersen and the Captain took the first hunter a short distance from the others in order to question him, it was my turn to ask questions. "What's that about, Anton? What was all that about warm fires and wood?"

"You live in a place where there are trees," Anton explained. "The only tree I've ever seen is a picture in your books."

"What do warm fires have to do with you seeing trees?"

"Let me ask you a question. Have you seen any trees since you left your Britain?"

I shook my head. "Anton, I really don't — "

He didn't let me finish. "Think of the *Fox*. What would it be if it wasn't for your trees?"

I thought about our ship. I pictured the deck — the wooden deck. And the wooden masts. Then I thought of the wood-panelled rooms, the wooden cupboards built into the wooden hull that was reinforced by wooden cross-beams.

"Wood is important on the *Fox*, no?"

"Of course it is," I said. "Without it, it wouldn't exist."

"Then think about what it means to people who live in a place where there are no trees at all. Wood is worth more than the metal that you wear on your fingers."

"More than gold?"

"The only wood for the Inuit is the driftwood that washes ashore. From this we must build our sledges and spears. Finding the drift logs is luck."

"So, can you imagine what it would be like to find a wreck? A whole ship? You'd have enough wood for everything. For a long, long time. Why, you'd even have wood to burn for warmth."

I smiled. "So Petersen was asking the hunters about warm fires to see if they have enough wood to burn. That would mean that their village knew of a wreck."

He nodded. "If I knew where a wreck was and someone asked me to tell, I'd say I didn't know. I'd want to protect my treasure."

12

March 2, 1859. Camped on the western coast of Boothia Peninsula, near the Magnetic North Pole.

We've traded for relics from the Franklin Expedition. We have a handful of silver knives and forks, a medal, a piece of gold chain and some bows and arrows carved from oak. The medal is marked "Mr. A. McDonald." The Captain told me that he was my uncle's assistant surgeon.

The Inuit claim that all of the relics come from an abandoned small boat on an island near the "salmon river," but no one seems to be certain where this place is. And of the *Erebus* and the *Terror*, there is only the skimpiest of information....

Our four hut-makers left at dawn. A few hours later they returned with the entire population of their village. I counted forty-five people.

The Captain assigned me several Natives to interview, including one older hunter named Ooblooria.

I asked him if he knew of any large ships.

He nodded his head. "A big ship. Three tall. It was crushed in the ice."

"Three tall?" I repeated.

He drew a ship with three masts in the snow.

"You saw this?"

He shook his head. "I didn't. I heard about it."

"Who told you?"

He shrugged.

"Someone of your village?"

"No, not from my village."

"Is the ship washed ashore? Did you get wood?"

"I didn't see it," he said. "I heard that the ship went under."

"Do you have anything from the ship you want to trade?"

"It went under before anyone got things."

"Did you see any white men? Did they go under with the ship?"

Ooblooria shook his head. "I heard that they were all on land."

"They got off safely," I smiled. I thought that this was good news. If the ship was damaged and the crew had made it safely to shore, it was possible that some of them could have built a shelter.

I tried to explore the connection between the small boat found on the island and the ship that had sunk. "The boat on the island, did it come from the ship?"

"I heard that white men dragged a boat from the big ship."

"Do you know what happened to the men?"

"I was told they all died. There were bones around a small boat near the salmon river."

"Do you have anything to trade from the salmon river?" I asked.

He nodded and called to one of the women. She shuffled over and handed him a long spear. He then gave it to me. "Good wood," he told me.

I examined it. It was made of oak. It could easily have been carved from a gunwale of a small boat.

"Where did you get this?"

"Same place as everything else. Salmon river."

"Where is the island? Which way would I travel?"

He pointed south, then shook his head and pointed southeast. "Maybe this way."

"That really helps," I mumbled in English. "How many days' journey?" I asked.

"One moon. Many days."

The other Inuit I interviewed had even less information than Ooblooria. I tried to trick them with the warm fires question that Petersen had tried on the hunters. But either they knew my motives, or they didn't have any wood.

The last person I talked to was a girl about my age. She was quite pretty, her skin a soft bronze and her smile just as soft. *"Pilletay. Pilletay,"* she began. That means, "Give me. Give me," and is the way bartering begins.

After I offered a small knife, she told me that she hadn't seen any wrecks during her lifetime. She didn't know of any Europeans. In fact, we were the first white people she'd seen.

And then she began to question me.

"Why do you tie your hair in knots?" she asked.

"It's just..." I paused. I didn't know the Inuit word for 'curly.' "That's just the way it grows."

"It grows in knots?"

"It's curly," I said.

"Curwee."

"Close enough," I told her. "Where do you find the wood you burn in the winter?"

"No wood," she shook her head. "Moss soaked in blubber. No wood. Are you white all over?"

"Pardon?" I said in English.

She looked as puzzled as I was. "Pardwon?" she repeated.

"What do you mean?" I explained.

"Under your clothes, is everything the same colour as your face?" she wondered.

"I...well..."

"You got a white belly?" she giggled.

"Let's talk about the wood."

"Already told you. No wood. You got a white behind?" The giggle turned into a laugh.

"Thanks very much." I stood up. "I don't have any more questions."

I returned to Captain McClintock.

"Any luck, Peter?"

When I told the Captain what I'd found out from Ooblooria, he confirmed that Petersen had discovered the same thing during his conversations. So it seems that either the *Erebus* or the *Terror* sank. But what of the other ship and the men? Is it possible that some of them survived?

13

March 4, 1859. Camped approximately thirty miles north of the Magnetic North Pole, west coast of Boothia Peninsula.

Last night I suggested to Captain McClintock that the little information we had received from the Inuit could mean that someone from the Franklin Expedition might have survived.

"How do you figure that?" he asked.

"Well, sir, the Inuit told us that the men of the *Erebus* or the *Terror* made it safely to shore," I pointed out. "I was thinking about that. What if something happened to us? Suppose we had to leave the *Fox*. What would we do? We'd start walking south, wouldn't we? Wouldn't we try to make it to the Hudson's Bay Territories?"

"We might," the Captain said. "Or we might walk north to try to find a whaling ship. It would depend on the circumstances that forced us to leave the ship. It would be different in an emergency. And it would be very different in the summer than the winter. It would depend on our food supply. Many factors."

"Well, sir, it appears that the crews of my uncle's ships tried to make it to the Hudson's Bay Territories. The 'salmon river' has to be on the mainland. It has to have enough fresh water to support a salmon run. That means a river on the continent itself."

"I'll agree with that," the Captain said. "We know that one ship is sunk. The Inuit tell us of a small boat on an island. This matches what Dr. Rae discovered. My guess is that the island is Montreal Island. And the river is Back's Fish River. But remember, according to the Inuit, the white men died. They found skeletons."

"But only a few. And there was only one boat. What if the others made it to the mainland and followed the river? They would have finally made it to the trees. They would have been able to build shelter and fires. There'd be game to hunt."

"It's unlikely that happened," the Captain said. "Not after all these years. If they did make it as far south as the forests, then they would have journeyed farther to a trading fort."

"But maybe not, sir. They may even have joined an Inuit village. They could be waiting for us now on the west coast of King William Island."

"Peter," the Captain explained, "nobody hopes that there are survivors more than myself. But let's be reasonable. Your uncle and his crew were the finest explorers. They were hand-picked from the entire Navy. If they had survived, they would have found a way to communicate with someone. Remember that we're the *fortieth* search expedition to look for them."

"But, sir — "

The Captain held up a hand to stop me. "They may have indeed been making for a trading fort. But I think the relics show us that they didn't complete their journey. My thoughts are that they starved to death."

"With all due respect, sir, that doesn't make any sense to me," I said.

The Captain turned to Petersen. "Our boy is getting more cheeky by the day."

Petersen smiled. "There *are* strange circumstances, Captain," he said.

"Exactly," I went on. "If they were starving, they wouldn't have bothered to take what they did. So they must have had food with them. Look at the things we traded. Silver forks. And knives. And Mr. McDonald's medal. When Rae traded for his relics, everyone thought the Inuit had been aboard the *Erebus* and the *Terror*. Now we know that they got them from the small boat — a boat that was being pulled on a sledge. The Natives found it a month's walk from King William Island. If the Franklin Expedition was starving, they wouldn't have bothered to take cutlery, would they?"

"And so you think that because they had time to take knives and forks, they had food?" the Captain asked.

"Yes, sir. And I think they went as far as they could with the small boat. Maybe they had to leave the boat to continue on foot."

"Just because we know they took cutlery doesn't mean they had food," the Captain reasoned. "We have no idea how big their food supply was. Remember that much of it spoiled and was left on Beechey Island. Their three-year supply may have been exhausted. We don't know what year this all took place. The fact is, your good uncle and his men would have found a way to make contact after such a long time. And how do you explain the skeletons the Inuit found?" He paused and yawned. "Now, let's get some sleep."

"I could be right, sir," I insisted.
"I said, let's get some sleep."
Well, I could be!

14

March 6, 1859. Camped approximately sixty miles north of the Magnetic North Pole, west coast of Boothia Peninsula.

As we were resting for our midday meal, Mr. Petersen came and sat next to me.

"You know, boy, I find it hard to believe there is anyone left alive as well. But there are a few odd questions." He unwrapped some frozen strips of fat from the bear he'd shot last autumn. He offered some to me, and I began to chew on a piece.

As we ate, we watched Anton and Captain McClintock examine the paws of the dogs.

"I could be right, Mr. Petersen. I don't see why they would bother to off-load knives and forks if they were abandoning their ship. Food would be first. And if they didn't have any food left, then why bother with silverware?"

"It is a good point," Petersen agreed.

"I think they took the cutlery because they thought they were going to be rescued. Either by the other ship, or perhaps by a search party. Silverware is useless if you're starving to death."

"I think we'll find out more in the spring," Petersen said.

The Captain came over to us, removed a mitt and asked Petersen for some bear fat. "You know," he declared as he stared at the grey substance, "I have actually developed a taste for this vile fat. In fact, I prefer it to pork." Then he looked at me. "I'm pleased with your efforts, Peter. When we make the journey in the spring to King William Island, I'd like you along."

Of course I'm delighted to go on the spring journey. But I tell you this, dear journal: if I hadn't been asked, I would have been more than shocked, and I would have protested most angrily.

15

March 15, 1859. Aboard the Fox, *frozen in the ice off Port Kennedy, Bellot Strait.*

We returned to the *Fox* as fast as possible, although stormy weather kept us hutbound for a few days.

Everyone aboard is in good health, except for Thomas Blackwell. Dr. Walker says that he has developed a serious case of scurvy.

What a luxury it is to sit in clean clothes and write this sitting at a mess-table in a warm and cosy ship. I never thought that the *Fox* would appear so inviting to me.

It was so pleasant to remove my clothes, as I hadn't been out of my parka and seal-skin trousers for a month. The rash from the lice is quite severe in a few spots. Dr. Walker gave me some cream to put on the bites.

"You're not sleeping below deck until you bathe," Thomas Grinstead threatened me. Needless to say, he wasn't the only person who was pleased that I decided to wash immediately.

Everyone commented on how much thinner we were. But besides a loss of weight, the only complaint from the members of the sledge journey is tiny, white scars on our cheeks, ears and chin. In addition, the Captain, Petersen and I have thick white calluses on our fingers. This is the healing of frostbite. It is interesting how nature takes care of us, because, despite being thinner and slightly frostbitten, we're in excellent health, without a sign of cold or scurvy. The Captain has ordered a double ration of lemon juice just in case.

It appears that our bodies have adapted to this terrible climate. We have become like the Inuit.

I think this is a good sign. If we are doing so well, then my uncle and his men could have adapted in a similar manner. Perhaps they're waiting in a comfortable place with plenty of game — waiting to be rescued.

16

March 19, 1859. Aboard the Fox, *frozen in the ice off Port Kennedy, Bellot Strait.*

Thomas Blackwell is bedridden with scurvy. He has all the signs of that disorder: weakness, depression and bleeding from his gums. Dr. Walker is extremely concerned.

Anton and I shot two ptarmigan today, but still no seals. The weather was quite pleasant, near freezing, and we walked for many miles along the shore.

We have been hunting almost every day since our return from the sledge journey to the Magnetic Pole. After those four weeks of activity, I've found it difficult to adjust to the routine of the ship. I don't seem able to stay still. I rush through my chores and then grab a musket and tromp across the land for the rest of the day. It's the only way I can feel relaxed.

The sledge journey around King William Island is due to leave on April 2. It would be silly to pretend that we're not anxious to be underway, but this time our reaction is a little different. Before we were more like young children waiting for a birthday pudding. Now we have a quiet confidence. We really are close to our goal, and everyone knows that.

I had an interesting talk with Anton before we went hunting. We were feeding the dogs. Anton was checking the paws on one of the females. When we returned, her front feet were so damaged that I thought we'd have to destroy her. Now there is well-healed scar tissue. It's amazing how hardy these northern dogs are.

"Anton, remember the Inuit we talked to on the sledge trip?" I asked him. "Why is everyone's memory so poor? No one seems to remember much about anything. Nobody could tell us where the salmon river was. Nobody knew where the wrecked ship was. Why?"

Anton began checking the paws on another dog. "You have to remember that these people are wanderers. They follow the seals and fish. Some villages have favourite places they may return to every year or so, but most of the time they move over a large area, maybe returning to one place every five years or more."

"Wouldn't it be worth remembering where the small boat was?"

"Only if there was a good supply of seals or fish," Anton answered. "You know we do not remember the number of years that have passed. Suppose it happened a long time ago. Since then you've made many summer camps and gone off exploring twice as many times. When you try to remember a certain spot, the memory can be a little mixed up, no?" He pointed at his forehead. "Different people can remember it a different way."

"I think I'd remember," I told him.

Anton stood up and stretched. "That's because you British think it is important to record all kinds of useless things. I see you writing in your book. I see your officers doing the same thing. To my people, the most important thing is how we will eat tomorrow."

"I still can't really understand that," I said.

"And I still can't see how you British eat those biscuit things," he grinned. "Now that I have explained something to you, perhaps you could do the same for me."

"As long as you don't ask me about our deafness," I said.

"No, it's not that. I want to talk about women."

"Women?"

"Females."

"I'm afraid I don't know much about...women."

He laughed. "I don't really want to talk about women. I want to talk about the lack of them. Why are there no females on the ship? Why do you travel without your wives?"

"Well, I guess because there's a tradition that females aren't allowed on ships."

"Why?"

"There's the difficulty of privacy," I explained.

"Privacy? What is that word?"

"A separate place. A separate room like the Captain has. You can't have men and women using the same toilet bucket or sleeping on the same deck."

"Why not?"

"Because men and women don't do that."

"Why not?"

I sighed. "It's just the way we do things."

"Isn't it natural for men to want women with them?"

"Of course."

"But you say one of the reasons you do not have females on the ship is because you'd have to keep them separate from the men."

"I know it sounds strange, but that's more or less true. Besides, if there were girls on the ship, we'd be more interested in them than in our duties, wouldn't we? I can't imagine what I'd do if Elizabeth was on board."

"You would enjoy her company," Anton suggested. "Then you wouldn't be thinking about her all the time because she'd be here. I have seen you looking at no-place in the distance. You are thinking about her, no?"

"Not really," I said defensively. "I'm just...I guess I do think about her a fair bit."

"So you think about the females whether they are here or not? This is most confusing."

"I don't think I'm explaining it properly. There is another reason."

"Maybe I'll understand that," he said. "What is this other reason?"

"That's simple," I smiled. "It's because females aren't as strong as males. We could never ask them to put up with the conditions of this expedition."

Anton stared at me. "Females aren't as strong?" He began to laugh. "They're not as *strong*?"

"What's funny about that? Everyone knows that girls are more fragile than men."

He laughed louder. "I can't wait to get back to my village and tell my women that you British think they are weaker than men. It is a joke, no?"

"I'm not joking."

His laughter wound down. "Your women are not strong enough to have the babies, prepare the meat, make the clothes, keep the fire and carry the supplies between campsites?"

"Not in the way you're thinking," I told him. "I can't picture my Aunt Anne or Elizabeth doing those things in the way you're thinking."

"So when you pick a wife, you don't think about her strength?"

"No, that's not important."

"What is?"

"You have to be...attracted to them. You have to find them pretty and fun to be with."

"Fun to be with?" He repeated the phrase a few times as if he was trying to decide exactly what I meant. After a moment, he asked. "What good is fun to be with when you've got ten caribou to butcher?" He shook his head. "We have to stop having these talks, Peter."

"Why?"

"Because every time you explain something to me, I end up knowing less than before I asked."

We both laughed at that.

The conversation has made me miss Elizabeth even more. I tried to imagine how she may have changed over the past year and a half.

When I left she had already begun to grow into a young woman. And her hair was turning from carrot red into a deep copper. I hope that she hasn't cut it. By now it must be past her waist.

In a way, Anton is right. I do think of her most of the time.

17

March 23, 1859. Aboard the Fox, *frozen in the pack ice off Cape Kennedy, Bellot Strait.*

After a week of decent weather, a terrible storm kept us shipbound for the last four days. It was a return to the cold of Brand's funeral. The wind pushed freezing claws throughout the ship, and I had to sleep in my parka.

When I woke up this morning, I heard the howl of the air against the housing. But an hour later, the wind suddenly stopped, and we are now blessed by cloudy but more agreeable weather.

"The stink of these lamps gives me a headache," Anton said after breakfast. "Let's go for a walk on the ice."

"I have my chores," I told him. "You know I have to clean the officers' rooms. I can't go hunting until later."

"Just a short walk," he suggested. "We won't bother to take the muskets."

"A half hour, then," I agreed.

The dogs didn't share our desire for a walk. When we tried to coax a few of them to join us, they refused to move. They remained on deck, curled in the hollows they've scratched in the snow.

We must have journeyed about a mile from the *Fox* before we turned around. It was slow going.

This late in the season, the ice has been crushed into ridges. At times the footing was difficult.

"Tell me more about your uncle, Sir John Franklin," Anton said.

"I've already told you everything we know. He and his two ships with one hundred twenty-eight men disappeared over ten years ago. Except for the few relics that we and Dr. Rae have traded, and the graves on Beechey Island, there hasn't been any trace of him."

"I don't mean the mystery. I mean, tell me about him. What was he like?"

"I never met him. But whenever my parents talked about him, it was always with respect."

"Then he was a great man?"

"One of the most popular people in England."

"He must have been," Anton reasoned. "To have so many men follow him is truly great, no? And to have other men still looking for him so many winters later..."

"We're very close to finding out what happened."

"Perhaps he reached the edge."

"The what?"

"The edge," Anton explained. "I've heard stories of a place on the edge of the world which is so cold that when a man takes a breath, his whole body freezes. Maybe those men found the edge of the world."

"There is no edge of the world," I smiled. "The world is round like the moon."

"But the moon changes shape. Sometimes it has a edge."

"The world is round," I insisted.

"Then perhaps they sailed into the place of the spirits."

"No. Something happened to them that isn't part of a legend. Something real. That's what we're here to find out." I gazed over the ice at the black dot of our ship.

For some reason I turned around again to glance out to sea. I watched the rough seascape for several seconds before I focused on a piece of pack ice squeezing upward.

"That's strange," I pointed out. "That piece of ice seems to be heaving very quickly."

Anton turned, squinted and followed the direction of my finger. He and I realized what it really was at the same time.

"Bear!" I called in English.

"Nannook!" he shouted in Inuit.

We bounced off each other and began a mad rush back toward the *Fox*. After stumbling and tripping for a hundred steps, my boots flew out from under me, and I landed savagely on a ridge of old ice.

The breath rushed from my ribs. I tried to pull it back in, but nothing happened. Instead of inhaling, I made a sorry moan.

"Get up!" Anton glanced over my shoulder as he pulled at my sleeve.

I groaned at him.

"Nannook!" he said, as if I wasn't aware that we were being chased.

I groaned again. This time a little air passed down my throat. A wave of nausea came and vanished. I took a breath without making a noise.

Frantically I struggled to my hands and knees and then to my feet. I sucked in rapid lungfuls and glanced back at the bear.

It had closed on us rapidly. It was a giant of a

polar bear, a huge white monster padding swiftly across the uneven ice.

Anton pulled me so hard that I almost lost my balance again. We resumed our panic race back to the *Fox*.

"We should have brought a musket," I panted.

"A spear," Anton added.

Another glance over my shoulder revealed the white creature gaining quickly. We'd never make it back to the ship before it caught us.

"I thought you said that you've never seen a polar bear attack a person," I panted.

"I just said I've never *seen* it," he puffed back. "That doesn't mean I've never heard of it."

"Help!" I screamed in the direction of the ship. Maybe there was somebody on deck. Somebody with a gun.

"Help!" Anton added.

The ridges of ice absorbed our calls.

Behind me, I heard the bear snuffle. I didn't have to look to know that it was very close.

Some part of me was wondering if my parka would offer any protection from the attack. I quickly realized that as soon as the bear caught me, it would be over. Last October, before we froze in the ice, we watched a bear kill a grey seal on a piece of pack. It simply lifted the creature into the air with its massive jaws and shook its prey a few times to break its neck. It took only seconds.

Anton and I turned to look at the bear together. And then we stopped at the same time. There was no point running anymore.

The huge creature halted less than ten steps away. It lowered its head, snuffled once more and appeared to concentrate on us. Perhaps it was waiting to see what we would do next. Or perhaps it was merely deciding who to kill first.

Then it loped a little to the right. The breeze carried the smell of its bearness, a musky animal odour.

"It's going to attack from the side," Anton said.

"Why my side?" I protested.

"If it attacks, pretend you're dead. I heard a story once..." Anton stopped in mid-sentence.

The bear twisted its head quickly to the left. Its black nostrils twitched. It glanced at us for a moment and again looked to the left. Slowly, but with impressive grace, the animal raised itself and peered over the ice peaks.

"It smells something else," Anton said.

"A seal," I prayed.

"No." Anton shook his head and broke into a wide smile. "Dogs."

Ten huskies poured among the ice mounds. As soon as they saw the polar bear, they began to bark in a rapid fury. Again the bear glanced at us. Then it turned around and began a less graceful gallop away from the dogs.

"They must have caught his scent," Anton said.

The bear was quickly surrounded by a yelping army. Surprisingly, it hardly took notice. It merely increased the speed of its retreat.

A couple of the braver dogs tried to nip its back legs. The bear twisted around, growled angrily and thrashed at its pursuers with a front paw. One of the dogs squealed in pain and was lifted off the ice like a bird. It flew well above my height before smashing onto a section of flat ice.

That attack seemed to discourage the other dogs. They pulled back from the bear and, although they continued to shadow the creature's retreat, they had definitely lost enthusiasm for the chase.

Anton and I watched the monster and our dogs become spots in the distance.

The Greenlander was still smiling. "That was, as you say, a close shave."

"We're alive," I grinned. "We're still alive."

Anton jumped into the air and let out a whoop. "You're bloody right!" he said in English. "We're alive."

We hugged, slapped each other's back and tousled each other's hair as if we'd just won a game.

"You ever think of what it's like to be dead?" I asked.

"A place where it is warm," Anton said.

"No," I disagreed. "It's cold. Like this land. You know, one of my greatest fears is dying in the cold."

Anton thought about that for a moment. Then he stared across the ice. "You didn't have to worry about it this time. The bear would have eaten you. All up. You would have been warm. The inside of a bear is warm, no?"

Five hours after we returned to the *Fox*, the dogs came back. Four of the ten huskies had been wounded by the bear's claws. The cuts looked like they had been made by a knife.

18

March 25, 1859. *Aboard the* Fox, *frozen in the ice off Port Kennedy, Bellot Strait.*

Today Anton and I went walking on the pack ice again. This time we were armed. We discovered several frozen breathing holes, which meant that there were seals around. But no sign of the animals. I think I was half hoping to see another polar bear. A bear steak would be a pleasant change from the pemmican and ptarmigan.

"Peter," Anton said as he was checking an iced-over breathing hole. "I've been thinking about Franklin and his men and why they would leave the ships."

"And?"

"Well, what if they were like Mr. Blackwell?" he suggested. "What if they were sick?"

"Scurvy?" I said. "Dr. Walker told me that you get scurvy from lack of exercise and a poor diet. You see how Thomas Blackwell lives. He seldom goes on deck. He never hunts. He eats only the canned food. And I've noticed that he is more than fond of his grog."

"What if the men had poor food and they didn't hunt like we do? What then? Maybe they all got scurvy and left the ships to find better food and exercise."

I smiled. "I can't quite see that. Can you imagine them saying 'All right, we've all got scurvy. Let's go for a little run to Hudson's Bay Territories.'"

"Why are you grinning? What's the joke about that?"

"Sorry," I said. "It's just that I can believe that a few of my uncle's crew might have got scurvy. Maybe more than a few. But not everyone would have become sick."

"Maybe more had it than you think," Anton reasoned.

"All right, suppose that's the case. Then most of them would be like Thomas Blackwell. Look how ill he is. The last thing they'd think about would be walking across the Hudson's Bay Territories with silver knives and spoons."

"Then it could have been another sickness," Anton said. "I've heard stories of Inuit villages being almost wiped out because of a sickness. I've heard tales of white people making a trading visit to a village and two months later there are only a handful of people remaining alive. Maybe a sickness spread through the ships."

I thought about that. "You know, you may have something. They might have been sick. Not scurvy, but something else. Something like smallpox or a plague. Something that made it important to leave the ship. To get away from the sickness."

"But to ask your question, why take the silver spoons?" Anton wondered.

"Why, indeed? Maybe it was some kind of sickness that causes a high fever — a delirious fever. Maybe the men were so sick that they didn't know what they were doing."

When we returned to the ship, I immediately told this idea to Dr. Walker.

"I don't know any disease that would make them act oddly, Peter, outside of the rare case of apoplexy," he told me. "And that comes as a stroke. Quickly. With other serious symptoms."

"What about a high fever?" I asked. "I remember one time my uncle was ill. He had an awful fever and he raved about things that weren't happening."

"I imagine your uncle was bedridden?" the doctor asked.

I nodded.

"To have such a high temperature means that you're too sick to get out of bed," he told me. "Insanity is the only condition where people act in a bizarre way without being physically sick. It's hardly likely that everyone was insane, is it?"

"But taking the cutlery is so odd," I said.

"There may be a logical explanation," the doctor said. "We just don't know it yet."

"That's what Mr. Petersen told me. I thought maybe sickness was a logical explanation. Are you sure there's nothing else?"

Dr. Walker thought for a moment. "Outside of Hatter's Disease," he said, "there is nothing."

"Hatter's Disease?"

"It's a condition that sometimes afflicts the workmen who make gentlemen's hats."

"What happens?"

"Many complaints. Loss of appetite and weight. Stomach cramps. Numbness. Loss of muscle control. Poor memory. And strange behaviour."

"Why do only hatters get it?"

"Well, it's not only them," the doctor explained. "Workers in pewter factories sometimes suffer from it as well. The belief is that the metals get into the blood. You see, pewter is made of tin and lead. And hatters use mercury making headwear. It's thought that the metals get into the blood and poison it."

"I don't suppose they were making pewter on the *Erebus* and the *Terror*, were they?"

"Or hats," the doctor chuckled.

Still, I have a feeling there is something to Anton's idea. But what?

19

March 29, 1859. Aboard the Fox, *frozen in the pack ice off Port Kennedy, Bellot Strait.*

And yet another day on the ice. But with different results...

This morning, before beginning our hunt, Anton went to George Edwards, the carpenter's mate, to get a piece of dowling.

"What are you going to do with the pole?" I asked.

"Get a seal," Anton told me.

"Are you going to sharpen it?"

He looked at me as if I were a mad hatter. "There are seals around," he explained. "I think that they have so many holes in the ice that they're staying away from us. As we walk closer, they move away. We have to invite them back."

"With a pole?"

"Tonight, we'll have fresh meat," he said.

We walked east of the *Fox*. About a mile from the ship, we saw our first frozen breathing hole.

"Not this one," Anton said.

As I've written, a breathing hole is the space in the ice that a seal keeps open so it can surface to breathe. It scrapes new ice with its flipper to stop it from freezing. A single seal will have several holes.

Anton examined two others and rejected them as well.

By noon, the sun was so bright that I had to squint to stop my eyes from aching. Too many hours of sunlight reflecting off the ice and snow can cause temporary blindness. Dr. Walker says that it's extremely uncomfortable.

At last, Anton took a liking to a hole. He poked his knife into the ice and removed it with satisfaction. "Hasn't been frozen long," he said. "See, I told you there are seals around. They're just staying away."

He chopped at the ice with his knife to open the hole. Then he began to scrape on the ice next to the hole.

"What are you doing?" I asked.

"Under water, it sounds like a flipper clearing ice," he explained. "The seals will think it's another seal clearing a breathing hole."

I looked doubtful.

Then Anton stood up and grabbed the dowling. He placed one end in the water and put his lips against the other end.

"What are you doing now?" I wondered.

He didn't answer. Instead he started grunting and snorting at the pole. "*Arrup, hork, arrup, hurk...*"

"That's the stupidest thing I've ever seen."

Anton looked at me, but he didn't stop. "*Arrup, hirk, arrap, hork.*" He continued to kiss the pole.

I started to laugh. "Anton, that looks ridiculous."

"*Arrup, hork, arrap...*"

"Will you stop doing that," I chuckled. "No seal is going to be stupid enough to come through that hole with you belching and burping into it."

"*Hurk, hirk, arrrup...*"

It took me several seconds to catch my breath. "Stop it," I said between chuckles.

He pulled the pole from the water, placed it gently on the ice and picked up one of his spears.

"You don't really think that a seal is going to —"

Anton shushed me. He spread his legs on either side of the hole and stood frozen. He held the statue-like stance for several seconds. Very slowly, he began to lift his spear arm above his head.

More seconds passed.

And then a grey head popped to the surface.

Anton's arm dropped quickly. There was a sharp squeal as the spear point entered the seal's neck. Just as quickly, he grabbed the spear with both hands and yanked the animal onto the ice.

The animal thrashed once and then lay limp. Anton looked at me and smiled. "Now, what were you saying, Peter?"

"I...well...I don't believe..."

"You want to try it? We'll find another hole."

I shook my head. "No, I can't burp like that. It wouldn't be the same..." I paused. "Anton, that was unbelievable."

He smiled proudly. "I was born a friend of the seal spirit."

"And a friend of the belching spirit," I added.

An hour later, Anton found another hole he liked and repeated his unique hunt. Again a poor creature popped its grey head into the air and received a sharp spear for its curiosity.

The Captain, crew and dogs were extremely happy when they saw us dragging the seals back to the ship. It was too late in the day to prepare the animals for supper, so we're going to have seal steaks and liver for breakfast. After you clean the animals, you have to wash the flesh three or four times to get rid of the blubber. Think about eating butter that has been left in the sun for a week with a thousand flies having a party in the melting mess, and you have an idea of what seal blubber tastes like.

But if it's cleaned, it's better than beef. The first time I discovered the taste of fresh seal liver, Anton watched me eat several mouthfuls with interest.

"What are you looking at?" I asked.

"You."

"Why?"

"Because you seem to be enjoying yourself."

"I am," I told him. "This is great."

He nodded, but he was obviously confused.

"What's wrong?" I asked.

"It's dried," he pointed out. "It's warmed up. It's shrunk."

"It's been cooked."

"It tastes better raw," he said firmly.

"Raw? You mean, still bloody?"

Anton smiled and nodded. "Next seal we catch, you'll have to try some raw stuff."

"Stuff?"

"Fresh, warm, raw liver," he smiled.

Just the thought of it makes my stomach act like the ice sea — all heaves.

Concerning a more appetizing subject: My kit is now packed and secured on one of the sledges. We now only wait for Captain's orders to begin the final search. He has promised that we will be underway in a few days.

20

*April 4, 1859. Camped thirty miles south of Bel-
lot Strait, west coast of Boothia Peninsula.*

We're camped in a snow hut that we built on the
first journey. It is in remarkably good shape and
needed only minor repairs before we pitched the
tent over top for the roof.

The weather has been cold, well below zero, but
fortunately there hasn't been any wind to drive the
chill through our parkas.

Not much to write. On April 2nd, two sledge
parties of four members each left the *Fox*. Anton
and I are with Lieutenant Hobson and Mr. Young.
The Captain has Petersen, Thompson and
Hampton with him.

We plan to travel together to Cape Victoria,
which we hope to reach by mid month. Our team
will then cross Ross Strait to explore the west coast
of King William Island. The Captain is going to
travel south to Montreal Island at the mouth of
Back's Fish River in the hope that this may be the
island and the "salmon river" the Inuit talk about,
and that more relics can be discovered there.

I am pleased to be going with Lieutenant
Hobson. It's a noble gesture for the Captain to let
his First Mate lead the exploration of King William

Island. Obviously we have the better chance of making a major discovery.

I wish I could go to sleep and wake up three weeks from now on the coast of King William Island. I am anxious, excited and eager at the same time.

21

April 9, 1859. Camped fifty miles south of Bellot Strait, west coast of Boothia Peninsula, hut-bound in a storm.

Once again a fierce gale has stopped our progress. Although everyone is anxious to move on, I think we're all glad of the rest, especially Lieutenant Hobson, who's been suffering from leg cramps. The good weather I wrote about in my last entry lasted until the next morning. For the past five days we have been fighting a bitter and relentless wind.

My nose, lips and fingers are frostbitten. It isn't serious, but it is painful. And my eyes are inflamed from the glare and the snow and dust which is whipped from the ground.

I feel that I'm doing my weary body a much-needed favour.

Today is Elizabeth's birthday. She was fourteen yesterday. I wonder what presents she received?

I can recall the day of her tenth birthday....

Rachel and I had been living with my Aunt Anne less than a month when Elizabeth turned ten. My aunt had made a big fuss, a goose dinner with butter pudding as afters. Elizabeth's birthday present was a pink bonnet with red silk roses sewn on it. I pretended to think that such a hat was extremely sissy.

Even at that time, I was quite affected by Elizabeth. However, being still only ten myself, I didn't understand what I was feeling. But I did think it would be a good thing if I gave her a personal gift.

I had secretly carved myself a catapult, which I hid behind the shed in the back garden. Secrecy was necessary, because I knew that my aunt wouldn't allow me to own such a fine slingshot. Why not make a gift of so valuable a weapon to Elizabeth?

I coaxed her out back and made my presentation. She held the catapult between her thumb and first finger as if she didn't know what to do with it.

"Do you like it?" I asked. "Isn't it a jolly catapult?"

She looked at it as if it was going to bite her. Then she narrowed her eyes and stared at me. "Peter Griffin," she said in a shocked voice, "where did you get this?"

"I made it," I boasted. "I carved it from willow. The rubber I stole from the gin cases behind the pub."

"You stole it?" She sounded more shocked.

"Not really stole. I borrowed it. It's only strapping. They throw it away."

"My mum will kill you when she finds out you have this."

"But it's yours now. It's a birthday gift."

"I don't want this," she snapped. "What would I do with a catapult?"

"Kill birds," I suggested.

She threw it on the ground. "That's disgusting."

"All right, you don't have to kill birds. Use it to donk a cat."

"How can you even think things like that?"

I picked it up and held it out for her. "Use it for target practice, then. It's my gift. You'll have lots of fun with it. Look." I reached down and picked up a round pebble. "See the pillow case on the wash line? Watch this."

I straightened my arm, placed the stone in the pocket, pulled the rubber back to my face, took careful aim — "Watch this. This is fun — "...and missed. The pebble flew over the pillow-case target and smashed my aunt's kitchen window.

"Oh, my," Elizabeth gasped.

I was so scared of the caning that my uncle would give me that I dashed from the back gate and hurried down the lane.

It took the rest of the day and an empty stomach before I finally worked up the courage to return to the house. I expected a licking as soon as I walked through the door. To my surprise, my aunt welcomed me to the supper table with the question. "Do you know of any boys who have a catapult, Peter? Somebody broke one of our windows today. Your uncle George isn't half angry."

At the time, I was pleased that fate had spared me — fate and my cousin Elizabeth. She hadn't told her mother it was me.

Now, I wonder if Aunt Anne knew the truth. I'll have to ask her when I return. And I'll give her some money for the window from my wages.

Anyway, happy birthday, Elizabeth.

If all goes well, I'll see you again in the fall.

22

April 18, 1859. Camped north of Cape Victoria, Boothia Peninsula.

A most interesting day!

We met two families of seal-hunting Natives around noon. We immediately began to question them about any relics they might wish to trade. I was talking to a hunter called Oonalee.

"Do you have anything to trade?" I asked. "Anything that belonged to white men?"

Oonalee nodded and handed me a cutlass. It wasn't a complete sword, just half the blade. The steel had been sharpened into a new point.

"Where did you get this?" I wanted to know.

"I traded for it," he told me. "Traded with someone from a village on the island."

"From what island? From King William Island?"

That obviously didn't mean anything to him. He told me his word for it and then waved to the southwest. "The big island. That way."

It had to be King William Island. "When did you trade for it?"

He held up six fingers, then eight. "This many winters."

"The man you traded with. Where did he get it?"

"He told me he picked it up on a beach," Oonalee explained. "He said that it was longer and he broke it to make a knife."

"Was the beach on the big island?"

He nodded. "Near where a ship was on the beach."

"A ship?" I could hardly restrain my excitement. "A big ship?" I drew three masts in the snow.

He shrugged.

"Do you know anything else of the ship?" I asked.

Oonalee nodded and pointed at a pair of scissors I had to trade. He wanted to make a deal before continuing. I handed him the scissors and held three needles in front of me. "Tell me all about the ship. Everything."

He nodded as he studied the scissors. "There were two ships. One sank. The other washed on the shore."

I called the Captain over and quickly told him what I'd found out.

"Can he tell us where?"

I asked the question and the old Inuit nodded. "Ootloolik."

"Doesn't mean anything to me," the captain said.

"Is the ship still there?" I asked.

"The man I traded with says it was much broken. And many villages have taken wood."

I translated for the captain.

"Does he know the fate of the crew?" the captain wanted to know.

"Do you know of any white men, dead or alive?" I asked.

"The man told me that there was one body on the ship, all bones. He had long teeth," Oonalee explained as he reached over to take the needles.

I held them away from him. "What else?"

"I heard that many white men were dragging boats down to large river. Next winter, their bones were found there."

"Did they all die?"

He shrugged.

"Which way is the river?"

The Native pointed south and took the needles from me.

"You've been writing for a long time," Young just said to me.

"Recording what we found out from Oonalee, sir," I told him.

The Captain asked me to pass him some tobacco. He lit his pipe and agreed that the old Inuit was a great source of information. "So what do you think, Peter?"

"It seems that my uncle and his crews abandoned their ships somewhere off the west coast of King William Island. They were walking south to the Territories as we thought. It seems that many might have died."

"I think that *all* is a better word," the Captain said.

"But Oonalee wasn't sure of that," I pointed out. "And it still doesn't answer why, does it? *Why* did they leave the ships?"

And why did they take spoons, knives and forks, I wondered?

23

April 29, 1859. Camped at Cape Felix, King William Island, waiting to begin final search.

Yesterday the two sledge parties split up. Captain McClintock continued his southern journey while we marched directly across Ross Strait.

We have yet to begin our search of the west coast of King William Island, though. Both Lieutenant Hobson and Mr. Young are sick.

Mr. Young has a terrible case of snowblindness. It's a condition that has been plaguing all of us for several weeks. Unfortunately, Young's eyes are viciously inflamed, and he is completely without sight. He lies in his bag with an arm covering his face, moaning. Lieutenant Hobson says it will be several days before his sight returns.

As to the Lieutenant himself, he has pains in his legs and complains of muscle stiffness. We suppose this is scurvy, but he has been eating the canned pemmican and fresh game — the best of food, the same as the rest of us. And our daily march is certainly vigorous exercise. His activity and diet should prevent the illness. I'm thankful that I remain healthy.

To tell the truth, I would much rather be marching than writing. The wait is frustrating. I'm more than ready to explore the coast. I know I've written it many times before, but this time it is true. We *are* close.

24

April 30, 1859. Camped at Cape Felix, King William Island, preparing for final search.

Lieutenant Hobson's legs are still troubling him. They're so painful that he can't walk very far. And Mr. Young hasn't regained any sight yet. He says that his eyes are more comfortable today, but he's still unable to tolerate any light.

This means that Anton and I are going to begin the search of the west coast of King William Island by ourselves. Lieutenant Hobson has ordered it.

After dinner today, he told me his reasons. "Peter," he began. "Tomorrow morning I want you and the Greenlander to take one of the sledges and begin to travel southward."

"But, sir, we must wait for you to recover. Our mission is too important."

"Exactly," he told me. "I'm not sure when I'll feel healthy enough to carry on. And Mr. Young will need another day or two to recover. You know that time is of the essence. Summer isn't far away. Returning to the *Fox* will be difficult when the snow gets too soft. And we must be back in time for the break-up."

"But, sir — "

He stopped me. "Listen, you must start the journey. If, in a few days, Mr. Young and I are feeling better, we'll follow. But if we aren't, then it's most important that someone explore the coast. I'm afraid that, at this time, you are that someone. Do you understand, Peter?"

"Yes, sir."

He nodded. "You know what we're looking for. I want you to bring back any relics that you are able to carry. Any that are too large or too numerous, I want you to record. List everything. I understand Dr. Walker taught you the elements of navigation and mapping?"

"Yes, sir."

"Then I'm going to ask you to draw the coastline you travel over. Keep the best record that you can."

"Dr. Walker taught me how to grid."

"Good, good," Hobson went on. "And remember to be particularly alert for cairns."

"I know that, sir," I told him. "I know how important it is to check any pile of rocks. I'll make sure to check inside and to dig in the ground beneath."

"Good. If the Inuit story about the men leaving the *Erebus* and the *Terror* and walking down the coast is true, then it's only logical that they would erect a cairn to leave a message."

"I hope we'll find something, sir."

"So do I, boy. But the problem with a cairn is that it's also a signal to the Natives." The Lieutenant frowned. "They'd start tearing it apart in the hope of finding something valuable. Any piece of paper would be left to blow away. But you must check them anyway."

"I will," I told him.

"Be especially observant for old cairns," Hobson went on. "The stones will appear weathered. There will be lichen and moss growing in the sheltered cracks."

I knew this.

"If you find anything important, erect a new cairn and leave a message for us."

He handed me a chart and unfolded it. The map of King William Island was a vague outline with some detailed sections. He pointed to a spot on the southwest side of the island. "The west side is not completely mapped, but I don't think you'll encounter any major obstacles. If I don't catch up to you, you are to go as far as Cape Herschel. Then I want you to return northward. Do you have any questions?"

"No, Lieutenant," I told him. "You can count on me."

"I know I can," he smiled. "If I didn't, I wouldn't be sending you out."

"Sir, is there anything I can do to make you more comfortable?"

He shook his head. "Thank you, Peter. This scurvy is a terrible thing, but with rest, I'll be back on my feet."

There is part of me that doesn't believe it has come to this. Fate has given me a great honour and a great responsibility. When we set sail to discover my uncle's fate, I never thought the burden of the search would fall onto my shoulders.

If there is anything to be discovered, it will be me who finds it.

25

May 2, 1859. Camped at Victory Point, King William Island, on the search for Franklin relics.

Incredible! There is no other word to describe what has happened.

It isn't even dinner time, but Anton and I have pitched our tent. I must write down what we've found. We've discovered things of great importance. My hands are still shaking. At last, we have definite evidence of the fate of my uncle, Sir John Franklin, and his crew.

Where do I begin?

About two hours after raising camp this morning, Anton and I noticed a small rise close to the shore at Victory Point. What struck us as unusual about this slight elevation was that it was darker than the normal snow and grey rock. When we walked closer, I was shocked to discover that the rise wasn't land, it was a mound of clothing — a pile over four feet high!

For a moment, both Anton and I were too stunned to say or do anything. We simply stared at the assortment of trousers, shirts and jackets. When I began a closer examination, I discovered it all to be sailors' warm clothing.

"What is that doing here?" Anton asked.

"I don't know," I said.

"Do you suppose it comes from the two ships we're looking for?"

"It has to be," I answered. "This is from the Franklin Expedition. This is what thirty-nine search voyages have been looking for. It looks like it was just taken off a ship and left here. I guess they couldn't take it with them."

"Why would they take it off the ships, then?" he asked.

"Maybe they thought about setting up depots. Maybe they just didn't have time to do anything with it."

Anton waved his hand around the shore. "Look at everything else!"

Strewn about the clothing was a virtual sea of relics. Among the things we found are four cooking stoves, medicines, an empty meat tin with a split seam, iron barrel hoops, gun wadding, canteens, a two-foot rule, curtain rods, pickaxes and shovels.

"It's as if they took everything off the ship," Anton noted as he picked up a long copper rod. "What's this?"

The metal was coated with green oxide, but it was in remarkably good condition. "It's a lightning rod," I told him. "It's placed on top of the masts to protect a ship from lightning."

"Peter," Anton said in disbelief, "why would they bother to bring this with them?"

Why, indeed? If you were abandoning a ship, you'd take things that would help you survive. Not heavy cooking stoves or lightning rods. Or the silver cutlery that we traded for last March.

And then we spotted a small pile of stones a short distance down the shore. It wasn't an elaborate cairn. In fact, it was smaller than the pile of discarded clothing. We walked over and knelt beside it. The rocks were undisturbed. A fair growth of orange and grey lichen covered the sheltered cracks.

"It's old," I said. "It's been here a long time."

Carefully, I started to remove the top layer of stones. Then the second layer.

"Do you think it was put here by Franklin?" Anton asked.

I removed another layer of rocks. And another. As I pulled at the next level of stones, I saw the rusty metal cylinder.

"What is it?" Anton asked, as I removed the hand-sized can from the cairn.

"A tin cylinder. It's for leaving a message."

At one time the two sections of tin had been soldered together. But that solder had been broken and it wasn't difficult to pull them apart. A piece of rust-stained paper fell to the ground. I picked it up with unsteady hands and unfolded it. What a sad tale of the Franklin Expedition it tells....

There are two messages written on the paper. The first was placed by a Lieutenant Gore. It reads:

28 of May, 1847 — H.M. ships *Erebus* and *Terror* wintered in the ice lat. 70 N, long. 98 W.

Having wintered at Beechey Island, ascended Wellington Channel to lat. 77 and returned by the west side of Cornwallis Island.

Sir John Franklin commanding the expedition.

All well.

Party consisting of two officers and 6 men left the ships on Monday 24th May, 1847.

Gm. Gore, Lieut.

This short message tells us many things. First, it reinforces what we already knew — the expedition stayed their first winter at Beechey Island. It also tells us that my uncle tried exploring north of Beechey, up Wellington Channel and Cornwallis Island. They must have been stopped by the pack ice and returned south. Latitude 70 and Longitude 98 is northwest of King William Island. That is where the *Erebus* and the *Terror* froze during the winter of 1846-47.

This Lieutenant Gore and his expedition of seven were four days from their ships, making a foot search of King William Island during the spring weather of 1847, probably mapping it.

My uncle was alive and "All well."

So, two years after they left Britain, the expedition was doing fine. In fact, judging by the distance they'd covered, they were doing extremely well.

But there are two messages written on the paper. Around the margin of Lieutenant Gore's note is another story told in different handwriting. It reads:

April 25, 1848 — H.M. ships *Terror* and *Erebus* were deserted on the 22nd April, 5 leagues N.N.W. of this, having been beset since 12th September, 1846. The officers and crews under the command of Captain Crozier. Sir John Franklin died on the 11th June, 1847; and the total loss by deaths in the expedition has been to this date 9 officers and 15 men.

F.R.M. Crozier
Captain and Senior Officer
and start tomorrow, 26th, for Back's Fish River.

How simple this note is, how sad and how different from Lieutenant Gore's message of a year earlier. It answers more questions of the mysterious disappearance.

The *Erebus* and the *Terror* didn't manage to break free of the ice during the summer of 1847. They must have drifted farther south, because it only took Captain Crozier three days to reach the cairn and Lieutenant Gore took four.

How discouraging it must have been. To be stuck in the pack all summer as well as all winter.

My uncle died a few weeks after Lieutenant Gore had written his note. Nine officers and fifteen crewmen had also died.

I told Anton the contents of the notes and the questions they answered.

"It doesn't tell what made them leave the ships," he said.

"No, it doesn't, does it?" I looked at the debris. "Since there is so much here, we should make camp for the day. I'm going to have to record all this."

Besides my journal, I now have to make a list of all the objects found on the site. I'll also rebuild the cairn and leave information for Lieutenant Hobson in case he's following us.

Record the objects...

A few months ago, I held a brass button in the snow hut. At that moment, the Franklin Expedition became a real thing to me. Now I'm surrounded by it. There is so much of my uncle's voyage strewn on this beach.

It's as if I've entered a ruin and discovered the articles of famous people. A ruin that I'd only read about in a book. These clothes, the stoves, everything, was once used by people...my uncle and one hundred and twenty-eight souls. This is their property.

We've learned so much by this find, but there are still so many questions that puzzle me.

And part of me is stunned. There was always the hope that my uncle was still alive. Now, I must mourn for someone I never met. And I grieve more for my aunt, Lady Jane. When we return to England, she will be saddened by the news. I can only hope that perhaps it will come as a relief also — to know the fate of her husband.

26

May 4, 1859. Camped at unknown point, King William Island, on the search for Franklin relics.

There is no name for this point of land where we have pitched our tent. It isn't marked on the map. I'm the first European to walk this shoreline.

No, that's not true. Captain Crozier and the men from the Franklin Expedition travelled this same coast eleven years ago and probably Lieutenant Gore and his party the year before that. I wonder if they bothered to mark the shape of the land as I've attempted. Although I found the lessons interesting, I never thought that I'd use the skills Dr. Walker taught me for such an important task.

We haven't found any more relics or cairns. Of course, much of the ground is still covered with snow. We may have missed small things.

I've been talking to Anton about the find at Victory Point. For me, it seems to have asked as many questions as it has answered. It has told the details of what happened to the ships and the men, but it hasn't answered all the *why*s.

"Anton, I've been thinking about the things we found at Victory Point," I began.

"You wonder why they took lightning rods?"

"Yes, and the other stuff. I mean, it's now logical to think they had run out of food. It was the third summer; they only had three years' provisions. Some of the food had spoiled and was left on Beechey. So their supplies must have been almost exhausted. But why wouldn't they hunt?"

"I don't think there is much game around this land," Anton suggested.

"Why do you think that?"

"Because all that clothing and the metal is still there," he said. "The Inuit would have taken it if they had found it. If there haven't been any Inuit on this coast, then the hunting must be poor. We haven't seen any game at all."

"Maybe you're right. Let's suppose that, for whatever reason, the men on the *Erebus* and the *Terror* couldn't hunt. And let's suppose they had run out of food and were heading for the Hudson's Bay Territories. Why bother off-loading cooking stoves?"

"It's a puzzle, no?"

"A puzzle I've been thinking about since we traded for the silver knives and forks. But there are other things," I went on. "Lieutenant Gore reported 'All well.' Two weeks later my uncle, Sir John Franklin, is dead. It's obvious that he didn't die of starvation."

"It could have been an accident."

"That's probably the case, but it's an interesting coincidence."

"A *coincidence*." Anton stuttered the word.

"Sorry, I don't know your Native word. I mean, it's odd that it happened, isn't it? But more odd is Captain Crozier's note that nine officers and thirteen crewmen died."

"Why is that strange?"

"Well, I'm not sure about the crew of my uncle's expedition, but I imagine it was similar to ours. Of the one hundred twenty-nine men, I'd say thirty must have been officers."

"I don't understand what you're saying."

"In any crew there is one officer to every four or five crewmen. If the crew were dying of starvation or disease, then you'd expect that for every officer who died four or five crewmen would die. If nine officers are dead, isn't it logical that forty crew would have died? When you consider the numbers, whatever happened really hit the officers."

"Maybe it's just a *coincidence*," Anton offered.

"There's something else that puzzles me," I continued. "The note itself. Why did Captain Crozier write on top of Lieutenant Gore's message? Why didn't he use another piece of paper?"

"Perhaps he didn't have any," Anton suggested.

"I find that hard to believe. If they took barrel hoops, they surely would have taken paper. Crozier had pen and ink. Why not paper? And remember that his message was written in April. That meant he had to retrieve the cylinder, break the seal, thaw the ink and rebuild the cairn. Does that sound like he was starving?"

"Maybe they were stopped by a storm and he had the time to do this. Maybe they did forget paper."

"It is strange, though. It's very strange."

27

May 6, 1859. Camped at unnamed point, King William Island, on the search for Franklin relics.

We have made another major discovery. This time I'm so deeply disturbed that it is a chore to make this entry. Today's find is more dramatic than the cairn and relics at Victory Point.

Early this afternoon, we found a large wooden boat on the shore. I'd estimate it to be about thirty feet long and seven feet wide. Under the boat is a sturdy and very heavy oak sledge. There are thick whalelines attached to this sledge for the crew to haul the weight. The sledge and boat must weigh close to a ton, a terrible labour for starving men to pull.

More surprising than the boat and sledge are the articles we have found inside — another great quantity of clothing, eight pairs of boots, silk handkerchiefs, a toothbrush, combs, towels, soap, nails, saws, gun-covers, bullets, knives, rolls of sheet-lead, tobacco, an empty pemmican tin and twenty-six pieces of silver cutlery, to name but a few.

Most of this is just dead weight. If the men were dragging the boat to Back's Fish River, especially if they were in a weakened condition because of starvation or scurvy, why bother to drag articles that have little use for Arctic survival?

And other puzzles have been added. There is no rudder or oars — just six paddles. How did they expect to guide the boat up a river? And strangely, the sledge is facing north. It was being dragged back to the ships. It's as if the men decided that it wasn't such a good idea to leave the ships after all.

Indeed, the only indication of food in the boat, besides the empty meat tin, is a small amount of tea and about forty pounds of chocolate.

But the most startling discovery, both gruesome and compelling at the same time, is the two skeletons resting in the boat. One sits in the bow, the other aft.

Anton and I stood and stared at the bones for several minutes before either one of us could move. We were simply transfixed. I couldn't take my eyes from them.

When I held that brass button, I felt the reality of my uncle's expedition. It became more than a story of exploration. And today I understood that the Franklin Expedition was also made of flesh and blood. The search for survivors has always been a quest for faceless people, to find *someone*. Now I have met *someone* face to face. As I regarded their remains, I was seeing real people from the real expedition. And I understood that those real people were dead.

The skeleton in the front of the boat is a small person. It's been badly damaged. Perhaps wolves have taken part of it.

"This one was like you," Anton noted. "He was young. Maybe he was the boy, no?"

There were ship's boys on both the *Erebus* and the *Terror*. They were both younger than me when they set sail. I imagine that they felt as I had when they left Great Britain, excited to be part of such an important trip, yet afraid of their first time at sea.

And what did this boy think of the Arctic that first winter near Beechey Island? Did he suffer the homesickness that I felt? Did he complain about the chores? What did he think of the filthy toilet buckets, the lice, the cold, the oily lamps and the darkness? Did he help dig the graves of the three who died there? Did he dream of a sweet cousin half a world away?

What did he think when the ships didn't break free of the pack? When my uncle died? Did he help the doctor prepare the dead body? Did fear grab his insides when the order was given to leave the ship?

And how did it feel to be left in the bow of the boat. What was wrong with him? Scurvy? Starvation?

What could it possibly feel like to be left to die?

Is it any wonder that I'm so shaken?

The other skeleton is in better shape and is still clothed and covered with a wolf fur cloak. Beside it are two shotguns, each with a barrel cocked and loaded.

What was that poor soul protecting himself and the boy against? Bears? In it's lap, are five watches. I can only imagine that those who could walk left their valuables with this occupant in order to lighten their load on their return to the ships.

Whatever happened, they didn't come back to the boat. What a sad, strange tale.

28

May 7, 1859. Camped at unnamed point, King William Island, searching for Franklin relics.

Lieutenant Hobson and Mr. Young have joined us. I was more than pleased to see them. I've handed over the Crozier/Gore message to Lieutenant Hobson and made a full report. I'm pleased that I don't have the responsibility of these important finds on my shoulders.

Mr. Young is completely cured of his snow-blindness. In fact, he's in excellent spirits and very excited by the relics found at Victory Point and the boat and its contents.

Unfortunately, Lieutenant Hobson is still ailing. Although his walk is a little stronger, he cannot work for very long. Also, his gums are bleeding badly.

The Lieutenant has begun to catalogue the items on the boat. He's searched the pockets of the clothing and taken a close look at all the markings on the relics. Among his discoveries: Eight of the pieces of cutlery belonged to my uncle, Sir John Franklin, himself. They bear his family crest. From the markings on the rest of the knives and forks, it would appear they belonged to officers on the *Erebus*. Hobson has concluded that the boat itself is probably from the same ship.

The Lieutenant ordered Anton and I to clear the snow from the area around the boat, to see if we could find other relics. We found nothing.

When I discussed the puzzles with Hobson and Young, they both seemed curious, but so far they haven't made any theories.

Tomorrow we're going to start toward Cape Herschel. And I wish we were heading back to the *Fox*.

Now, even I understand there is no hope. My uncle is dead and everyone else on the Expedition is dead. This fact has brought back the feelings from George Brand's funeral. The empty, endless land has closed in on me.

Now that we have learned what happened, I want to leave. I want the green of Somerset, a sea of water and the warm smiles of Elizabeth.

29

June 6, 1859. Camped near Cape Adelaide, west coast of Boothia Peninsula, returning to the Fox.

Almost a month since my last entry. Our busy daily schedule has prevented more attention to these records. Also, Lieutenant Hobson is completely unable to walk. We are conveying him on the sledge. This has meant extra duties for the rest of us and no time for the luxury of my journal. I have no complaints about this. The labours give me little time to dwell on the fact that it is summer and the sea is still frozen. Now I wonder if the *Fox* will break loose from its prison in Bellot Strait. What will happen if we are beset in the ice for another winter like the *Erebus* and the *Terror*?

Briefly: We are camped by one of our food depots. The warmth has come quickly, the snow is soft and slushy and the sun is in the sky twenty-four hours. Today the weather is very mild, and we have camped early because of the sloppy snow. I hope tomorrow will be cooler. We would like to be making faster progress for the sake of the Lieutenant's health. And just to leave here.

We found nothing at Cape Herschel. There was a large stone cairn erected by Simpson on a voyage to find the Northwest Passage before my uncle's last attempt. Surely Crozier and crew would have seen this on their journey south and considered it a good place to leave records. The cairn, however, was in ruins, as if the Natives had searched it for valuables. If there was anything there, it is long gone.

We found no other relics on King William Island, but Lieutenant Hobson collected some from the boat and at Victory Point to take back to England.

When I brought Lieutenant Hobson his supper, I found him sitting up in his sleeping bag and writing in his log. "Are you feeling better, sir?" I asked.

He nodded. "My legs ache, but I'm in good spirits this evening. The best I've felt in weeks. The worst part about this scurvy is the depression."

"It puzzles me why you're suffering, sir."

"I know," he nodded. "It seems that the exercise and good food don't prevent this illness. There must be something else missing from our diet."

Mr. Young noticed I was writing in my journal. He asked me to remove a page and write a note to Captain McClintock who should be about one week behind us. This is what I wrote and placed in a small cairn:

June 6, 1859
Trust all is well. We are making haste back to the *Fox*. We hope you have found our messages telling about our finds on King William Island. After leaving that island, Lieutenant Hobson fell seriously ill with scurvy. In fact, he is unable to walk without assistance. He is being conveyed upon the sledge. Mr. Young is pushing as far as possible each day to get him

under doctor's care, although travel today
was stopped by the slush.
God be with you,

Peter Griffin

30

June 14, 1859. Aboard the Fox, *frozen in the ice off Port Kennedy, Bellot Strait.*

We returned to the *Fox* on this morning. Dr. Walker immediately took Lieutenant Hobson under his care and has placed him on a diet of fresh duck, preserved potato, lemon juice and strong ale. The doctor has ordered each of us a double ration of lemon juice. He says that we're all showing the early signs of scurvy. Mr. Young and Anton complain of tender walking muscles.

"I feel fine," I told him. "My legs aren't stiff at all."

"Your mood, boy," Dr. Walker disagreed. "It's not like you to be so down in the mouth. You've just returned to the ship after two months and I've seen hardly a smile. A deep mood is as much a sign as aching legs."

My mood is because the *Fox* is still firmly frozen in the pack. I've taken a careful look and notice at least a yard of ice holding her tight.

A sad note to our return: Thomas Blackwell, the ship's steward, died five days ago of scurvy. According to Grinstead, "He just stopped eating and wasted away."

Blackwell is buried next to Mr. Brand.

31

June 20, 1859. Aboard the Fox, *frozen in the ice off Port Kennedy, Bellot Strait.*

Yesterday the Captain and his sledge team returned all well. He was unable to find any major discoveries on Montreal Island, but he did trade for some relics with Inuit in the southern lands. He brought back tablespoons and the handle of a dessert fork, among other things.

Lieutenant Hobson is much better and is now able to walk. Although still weak, he is performing all of his duties. I'm feeling more lively as well. Perhaps I did need the lemon juice and the routine of ship life. But I still fret for the break-up. The weather continues warm and the pack ice is full of heaves and ridges. Once or twice we've caught a glimpse of open water in the distance, but the ice quickly closes it over. The *Fox* remains solid. Each night I pray that our fate does not mirror my uncle's.

This morning the members of the sledge teams met to discuss the finds. The Captain noted that although we must take back word that Sir John and everyone died in the third year of their expedition, at least we can assert that by sailing down the west coast of King William Island, Sir John Franklin was the first to discover the Northwest Passage. We can bring that honour to his name and widow.

The Captain also told us that he plans to record the last days of those brave men this way:

— *Erebus* and *Terror* froze in the pack north of King William Island for two winters

— Sir John Franklin died and Captain Crozier took command

— the ships may have been severely damaged by the ice pack

— food ran out and the men were starving, many may have been suffering from scurvy

— in May 1847, the ships were deserted and the men tried to walk down the west coast of King William Island

— they were dragging boats with them because they intended to sail up Back's Fish River

— everyone perished

"That is obviously what happened," he told us. "It is what we will tell Lady Franklin."

"May I ask a question, sir?"

"Of course, Peter. Are you still wondering why they took the cutlery with them?"

"And the other useless articles like the stoves and the lead sheets? And what was the boat doing facing the wrong way? What about the clothing? Ink, but no paper? And the skeleton with the loaded guns — "

"Peter," the Captain stopped me. "I've been giving this much serious thought. It puzzled me as well. Now I think I can clear up your questions."

"Thank you, sir."

"If the ships were damaged in the ice, then

they'd start off-loading before the thaw. And they'd take everything. Even lightning rods. Who knows when they would come in use? Meanwhile, their food situation was getting worse quickly."

"So they left a lot of the things behind and started dragging the sledges to Back's Fish River?" I concluded.

"Exactly," the Captain said. "And it appears they seriously over-estimated their strength."

"You mean that at first they thought they could make it with all that gear?"

"That's right," the Captain went on. "None of the officers would want to leave their valuables. They'd want to bring their silverware. Did you notice that we didn't recover any ironwear?"

"True," Hobson noted. "There were no iron knives and forks. Nothing that a crewman would use."

Captain McClintock nodded. "I believe that the officers divided up their valuables among the men. They let the crew members use it as a means of saving it."

"That makes a good deal of sense, sir," Hobson agreed.

"As I said," the captain continued. "They made the serious mistake of over-estimating what they could drag or carry. They exhausted themselves. Does that make sense, Peter?"

"I think I understand."

"Good," he smiled. "It took a little thought, but it all fits now, doesn't it?"

I told him it did, but I'm still not sure.

32

June 26, 1859. Aboard the Fox, *frozen in the ice off Port Kennedy, Bellot Strait.*

Some good news. The ice around the ship has pressure cracks in it, and an area of open sea is cleared a few miles from us. The captain says that if the weather continues, we should be free of the ice in a few weeks. But at the same time I noticed that during supper last night, he and the officers were figuring how to ration our supplies in case we didn't get loose. It's obvious that the thought of another winter has occurred to them as well.

There's been a pleasant change in our diet. The other day, a mother bear with two cubs curiously wandered by the *Fox*. Foolish animals! The cubs made an excellent dinner, very much like veal. And the dogs seemed equally impressed with the meat of the older animal.

Captain McClintock's conclusions still don't sit well with me. There are too many loose ends, too many questions without a sensible answer.

Captain Crozier's note revealed that the expedition had come to a dire strait. But it's curious that Crozier felt the need to write over Lieutenant Gore's note to tell of their desperation, yet he wasn't desperate enough to order the dumping of everything that didn't help survival. Why did they drag silver spoons all the way to Montreal Island?

I agree with Captain McClintock. I think that they may have been starving and suffering from scurvy, but I also think that there was something else. It's as if the officers were confused and befuddled, not really understanding the consequences of their orders....

Why did more officers die than crew? Was there a disease? Was there something that was affecting the officers more than the crew? What? What happened?

33

July 15, 1859. Aboard the Fox, *frozen in the ice off Port Kennedy, Bellot Strait.*

Halfway through yet another month and still the ice holds us firmly in its grip. There is open sea on the horizon and Bellot Strait is completely clear. Unfortunately, the pack has drifted around us. The Captain keeps a cheery face and says that a westerly wind and another week of fine temperatures will set us free.

Yet he's ordered an end to the double ration of lemon juice to preserve the precious liquid, and he and Lieutenant Hobson have a plan to divide the preserved meat if another winter is necessary.

I try not to think of that possibility. After our finds on King William Island, I fear the same fate too much. Even confessing this thought to my journal has left me with sweating palms and shaking hands.

34

August 9, 1859. Free of the pack, off Fury Point under sail and steam, heading for Greenland!

Last night I woke suddenly around three o'clock with the feeling that something was wrong with the *Fox*. I was so startled that I fell out of my hammock. When I stumbled to my feet, the slight swaying threw me off balance, and I fell into Anton, waking him.

Still befuddled by sleep, I couldn't understand the nature of our danger at first. The rolling of the boat, the creaking of the timbers, the soft thuds of loose ice bumping the hull didn't register for a few moments.

And then I realized what had happened. I shook my friend's shoulders and grinned into his face. "We're free!" I shouted at him. "The *Fox* is drifting! We're free of the ice!"

My voice woke several other of the crew who immediately began to swear at me, until they understood my words.

"Yaaaaah!" I shouted to make sure nobody continued to sleep and, still in my underclothes, I ran up the hatchway to the top deck.

Sure enough, a south-westerly breeze was blowing the broken pack ice and our ship toward open sea.

"Yaaaah!" I screamed at the water. "We're free! We're free!"

Within moments I was joined on deck by the rest of the crew and officers, most half-dressed like me. And seconds later, there was much hooting, hollering and singing.

"Thank God," Captain McClintock proclaimed in a much relieved voice.

"We're going home," I yelled. "We're going home!"

The crew pleaded for an instant party and a special issue of rum, but the captain refused. "We have much work to do. Unfurl the sails and stoke up the boiler."

Right now, I think I'm giddy from lack of sleep. I'm so relieved. We're going home!

35

August 18, 1859. At sea, Lancaster Sound, out of sight of land, heading for Greenland.

I am feeling so grand today that I had to return to my journal, even though I don't have much to write about. We are in the middle of an ice-free Lancaster Sound under sail to Greenland. God willing, I am within a month of England and Elizabeth.

Lieutenant Hobson is almost completely cured, the crew is in good spirits, and everything is running smoothly.

Shortly after we broke free, Mr. Petersen shot a white whale, and we had a feast of good blood-meat. I think it tastes very much like seal, perhaps a little better. Anton was especially delighted to devour great quantities of its skin, which is a good half-inch thick. He says that it is considered a great delicacy among Greenland Inuit. I find it rather tasteless myself.

That's all, dear Journal. No, wait. I've been spending several hours each day doing a new chore. Since Brand's death, the Captain has assumed the position of Engineer. Guess who has become Engineer's Mate? Guess who shovels coal for the new engineer?

36

September 1, 1859. At sea from Godhaven, Greenland, returning to England.

We have spent five days in Godhaven bringing on supplies and painting the ship. Britain is now so close. I keep trying to picture what Elizabeth looks like. What will she think when she sees me? Three summers. Three long summers.

The day after we docked, I found Anton standing on the deck of the *Fox*, his wages in hand, staring at the ship with a certain sadness.

"Are you all off-loaded?" I asked him.

He nodded and held up the bag of coins. "And paid."

"What are you going to spend that on?" I asked.

"A rifle," he told me. "And maybe one for my brother. And..." He looked around the deck again. "...and I've become quite fond of some of your ways. I think I might buy some wood and build a house in town."

"Somehow I can't see you living in one place."

"Oh, I'd never do that," he smiled. "All summer I will hunt. But it would be good to have a winter home, no?"

"It would be fine," I agreed.

"And a woman to share it," he grinned. "And what about you, Peter Griffin?"

"I'm not sure," I told him. "I'm going to spend some time in Somerset with my aunt and sister."

"And Elizabeth," he added.

"Yes," I smiled. "Then I think I'll sign on a Navy ship. I want to spend my life at sea."

Anton nodded. "You will do well. 'Captain Griffin' sounds very natural. I wish you much good fortune." Then he pointed at the dogs, who sat on the rocks by the shore. They had been taken off the ship the day before and had promptly planted themselves on the rocks. It was as if they expected to come back on board at any moment, as if they regarded the ship as their home.

"When you sail away, I will be like the dogs." There were tears in his eyes. "I'll wonder why I am not on board. Why I'm not with my friend."

He sucked in a deep breath, then held out his hand. "Goodbye, Peter Griffin. I am glad that we shared some years. I am glad we found out what happened to your Sir John."

"I'm going to miss you," I told him.

"You have been like a brother. I will miss you, too."

I had to breathe deeply to stop the feeling behind my eyes. "Goodbye, Anton. Until we meet again."

"Or until the wind carries our spirits."

I watched him walk down the gangplank toward the dock. "Goodbye, Auglituk," I whispered.

About the Author

Martyn Godfrey was born in England and moved to Canada when he was eight. He has lived in various places in Ontario and Alberta and now lives in Edmonton with his two children. Godfrey began his writing career while he was still a teacher, but is now writing full-time. A popular speaker, he is able to keep in touch with kids through the many school visits he makes each year.

He has written many novels, including two books published by Lorimer — *Plan B is Total Panic* and *Baseball Crazy.*